PRAISE FOR *SIDLE CRE*

"She can write. Not an easy story but a deeply satisfying one."
　　　　—**Dorothy Allison**, author of *Bastard Out of Carolina*

"In a lesser writer's hands, Jolene McIlwain's hardscrabble characters could become one-dimensional, stereotypic, but her empathy is such that we never doubt our kinship to them and their ultimate concerns. These stories are artfully constructed and the writing vivid and precise, often poetic but never pretentious. *Sidle Creek* is one of the best story collections I've read in a long time."
　　　　—**Ron Rash**, *New York Times* bestselling author of *Serena*

"Jolene McIlwain is a master of the vividly imagined natural world and of complicated characters, young and old. Meals burned and letters went unanswered as I waited to find out if the baby would survive, which boy would win the fight, whether the deer had escaped in these suspenseful stories. *Sidle Creek* is a marvellous debut."
　　　　—**Margot Livesey**, author of *The Boy in the Field*

"In *Sidle Creek*, characters don't fall in love, they unearth it. And that's what these stories do, they unearth layer upon layer of love for life and all its hills and valleys. These are stories in which textures are beagle-soft; a creek can heal or at least make you believe it can; a calf can be a trigger to a violent memory and the cutest little thing;

a person can be a quartersawn board, which is to say stable, or they can be rift-sawn, which is to say not. These stories show life in all of its beauty and its horror."

—**Ayşe Papatya Bucak**, author of *The Trojan War Museum*

"Heir to the immortal ruralists of the American short story's halcyon era, Jolene McIlwain crafts fiction so close to the bone, with such an unflinching fearlessness of the soul's dark night, that she will restore your faith in what the short story can achieve in the hands of a born expert. *Sidle Creek* is a debut worthy of alignment with the best of Dorothy Allison and Daniel Woodrell."

—**William Giraldi**, author of *Hold the Dark*

"Welcome to the Pennsylvania of Jolene McIlwain, a world of strip mines, cockfights, deer hunters, Rolling Rock beer, and a cast of characters as memorable as any from Sherwood Anderson's *Winesburg, Ohio*. McIlwain's debut story collection, *Sidle Creek*, shimmers with the plain-spoken, and yet luminous, portrayals of its rural characters whose lives are made up of moments of grit and grace. How does she do it? How does she turn the ordinary into something magical, universal, and eternal? These are stories to savor for all they have to tell us about being alive."

—**Lee Martin**, author of the Pulitzer Prize Finalist, *The Bright Forever*

"Jolene McIlwain's *Sidle Creek* is a debut collection of stories that reads like the work of a seasoned master. Like Chekhov, she writes about her characters with both a cold eye and a warm heart, and as a result they and their conflicts and traumas come vividly and complexly to life. And her prose is so rich with sensory imagery that it allows us to see through the words as through a window into the world she describes, and that world, the brutal and beautiful world of western Pennsylvania's Appalachian Plateau, is so compelling it becomes virtually a character itself. This is a book, and an author, that should not be missed."

—**David Jauss**, author of *Glossolalia: New & Selected Stories* and *Alone With All That Could Happen: On Writing Fiction*

"*Sidle Creek* is a beautifully drawn collection that turns away from nothing in the pursuit of hard truths. Atmospheric and thrumming with life, these stories offer the ultimate gift—a chance to look within and ask our own difficult questions, and if we're lucky, offer ourselves the same hard-won understanding we can't help but have for these unforgettable characters. These are the stories that haunt them, the ones they can't help but tell, and that energy radiates off every page in evermore surprising and heartbreaking ways. *Sidle Creek* aches with the particular beauty of grief and is written with remarkable grace."

—**Chelsea Bieker**, author of *Godshot* and *Heartbroke*

"There's a subterranean wisdom threading through the ground of these stories, creating deep links, pulling stunning parts into a still more stunning whole. Jolene McIlwain gives us the kind of truths that can only come from knowing her subjects—people, animals, and landscapes alike—entirely and truly, in all their darkness and light. An extraordinary debut from a writer of rare insight and lyric power."

—**Clare Beams**, author of *The Illness Lesson*

"Author Jolene McIlwain shines in this debut collection of short stories showcasing her profound vision, authenticity, and compassion. These stories and characters will sear themselves in your mind and heart forever, such is the beauty and precision of McIlwain's prose, the deftness of her storytelling chops. Like Annie Proulx, this author intimately knows the places and people of her stories. Knows their secrets, their histories, their heartaches, and all-too-human failings. McIlwain brings to vivid life the unique world of rural Appalachia with wisdom and candor and an uncanny ear for dialogue. A masterful collection, *Sidle Creek* is only the beginning for a stunning writer we'll be hearing much more from in years to come."

—**Kathy Fish**, author of *Wild Life: Collected Works*

"The stories in Jolene McIlwain's *Sidle Creek* are dark and painful, atmospheric and heartbreakingly honest. Filled with characters struggling to survive in a setting as alive and rich as any I've seen, these stories are hard to read and harder to put down. I loved it!"

—**Kelly Braffet**, author of *Save Yourself*

JOLENE MCILWAIN

*sidle
creek*

STORIES

MELVILLE HOUSE BROOKLYN • LONDON

SIDLE CREEK

First published in 2023 by Melville House
Copyright © Jolene McIlwain, 2022
All rights reserved
First Melville House Printing: March 2023

Melville House Publishing
46 John Street
Brooklyn, NY 11201
and
Melville House UK
Suite 2000
16/18 Woodford Road
London E7 0HA

mhpbooks.com
@melvillehouse

ISBN: 978-1-68589-041-4
ISBN: 978-1-68589-042-1 (eBook)

Library of Congress Control Number 2022949584

Designed by Emily Considine

Printed in the United States of America

10 9 8 7 6 5 4 3 2 1

A catalog record for this book is available from the Library of Congress

"The Steep Side" originally appeared in *West Branch Magazine* in 2021; "Sidle Creek" originally appeared in *Aquifer: The Florida Review Online* in 2021; "The Less Said" originally appeared in *New Orleans Review* in 2018; "Seed to Full" originally appeared in *The Fourth River* in 2016; "Drumming" originally appeared in *Cincinnati Review*'s miCRro feature in 2017; "Sostenuto" originally appeared in *Litro Magazine Flash Fridays* in 2018 and in Best Small Fictions Anthology in 2019; "Steer" and "Shell" originally appeared in *Prime Number Magazine* in 2017 and 2021; "Oiling the Gun" originally appeared in Matter Press's *Journal of Compressed Creative Arts* in 2020; "Where Lottie Lived" originally appeared in *Northern Appalachia Review* in 2021; "Angling" originally appeared in FIVE, the *Pure Slush Anthology* in 2016; "Seeds" was a Top 25 Finalist in *Glimmer Train*'s Very Short Fiction contest in 2008 and originally appeared in *Janus Literary Magazine* in 2021; and "Loosed" received an honorable mention in *Glimmer Train*'s Short Story Award for New Writers in 2018.

For Ava, Muddy Myst, Lucy June, Tipper, Sydney, and my Hank

For all the squirrels, birds, possums, groundhogs, that one baby hawk, the three neighbor cats, the monarchs, mantises, and especially the whitetail deer who've shown up when I needed them most

For the one who reminds me to dig deep and to always go for the hole shot when the gate drops

and

For the earthling who calls me Mother Person

To the bottle in the ditch, to the scoop
in the oats, to air in the lung
let evening come.

—JANE KENYON ("LET EVENING COME")

CONTENTS

SIDLE CREEK

Sidle Creek

The first rock wall Esme Andersen built was in 1975 when she'd just turned twenty and was halfway through an engineering degree. Her father had been diagnosed with MS, and she was home from college for the summer. People said she was pregnant—"Look how bloated that belly is"—but she'd never been with a man. She just passed clots and passed out a lot. "That's why they scraped her out," Dad said. "Ended up taking everything. It's a pity, you know."

I didn't quite know.

Esme and her dad took trips to the creek bed every day for two weeks that summer, gathered up flat rocks from the slippery bottom of the Sidle to build the wall. The rumor was Esme kept adding stones on days she felt well, sometimes only a few—toiling over making the fit right, a half turn here and there. When she was poor and in pain, she claimed she felt the hum of protection within the kissing stones of her very own rampart.

After her father died, Esme ended up living alone behind that dry-stacked wall, being called strange, a fool. But I adored the wall, how it held.

~

Back when we first moved next to Sidle Creek—not a large creek but cool enough for trout—a man who'd been blinded by welder's flash got his sight back when he fell into its water. When Dad gave directions to our house he'd say, "Follow Sidle from the bridge near Colwell's Cemetery about three quarters of a mile out Stone Church Road. If you get to the old pump station, you got out too far." He'd add, "You won't see our house from the road, so just turn right where the creek takes a sharp bend to the left—where Prichard got his sight back—and you'll see our drive." How strangers could have been helped by his directions was lost on me, but no one questioned them, and every time someone said, "What do you mean got his sight back?" Dad would tell the story about how the Sidle's water cured Mr. Prichard.

~

Granddad had a bleed at the muddy bank of the Sidle the same year my mom left. His best fishing buddy, Lee, gave him sips of whiskey thinking it was a clot that could thin, but it was a different kind of stroke. "Hemorrhagic" read the death notice. Dad repeated the word three times, slow. Dad said Lee couldn't have known when he held the bottle's lip to Granddad's he was making his death come swifter. For a long time, he wondered what might've happened had Lee let Granddad drink some of the Sidle's water instead, but decided it was all good. "He didn't have to suffer years of half a life, unable to talk or walk or dance or fish. No one should have to suffer."

But when Granddad showed up in everyone's dreams, even the neighbors', he had dirt all over him. "Just that dried-out topsoil from trying to get back to us from his grave. Not the muddy silt from the Sidle," Dad said. "Don't you worry. He didn't fault the creek. He loved it pret' near as much as he loved us."

~

Before my uncle Bobby went away to the pen, back before his layoff at the mine and his broken marriage and the drug bust and the helicopters hovering over the hunting camp while state boys dragged him from the attic with bits of pink insulation stuck to his shirt, we all fished together at Granddad's spot, like some happy family. But the truth is my dad might have sooner just gone alone. We kids were too loud. Spooked everything. And Uncle Bobby used weird things for bait that day. Hot dogs, Pop-Tarts, bubblegum, carrots.

~

Late-season snow runoff, and a bout with the wrong side of manic, sent Miss Turner into the deepest channel of the Sidle with stones from the Allegheny River weighting her coat. "She'd given it some thought," Dad said. Those river stones were smooth and small—unlike the bulky, irregular creek stone covered up in the high-water rush—and she could fit them nicely into the woolen coat she'd sewn with extra-deep pockets, some said, exactly for this deed. Two anglers scouting for spots to stock rainbows tried to pull her from the high cold. One of the Colwell boys, a newly minted volunteer fireman who'd completed fifty-two of seventy-two passes in the final game of his senior year, overhanded a throw bag to each of them, landing the bags right at their chins. Still all three abided feverish shivering fits of hypothermia for a handful of days in the ICU. Miss Turner lived three more years before something like cancer nettled into her woman parts and offed her slow and terrible. Dad blamed Miss Turner for using the creek wrong. He blamed her for the fact that the browns weren't taking night crawlers that season. He swore her actions cursed the line, cursed the hooks.

~

Dad always said attractor dries were best for catching wild browns. I tried every fly in the box, every single one clatched to my hat. Caught my best brown once when the stream was high and thick after a hailstorm. Filled my waders, nearly drowned. I cried out for help but no one heard. "You got yourself out. Found good footing on that creek bed. That's what counts," Dad said, patting me on the shoulder, then hugged me tighter than he ever had in my whole thirteen years.

That night I dreamed I kept finding something stuck on the undersides of rocks, stuck to the slippery green of them, and how it stuck I couldn't figure; I worried it would tack over the whole run. It was stuck to everything. When I woke up, my panties were full of blood. I told Dad and he said, "That's natural. It's time. Go to Mom's closet and get her napkins in a pink box," and I did. They were right beside the pretty purses and shoes in boxes she'd left behind when she left me behind too, two years before. He said, "Let's go see how they're runnin' today."

I knew the blood would come. I'd learned about it a few years before. I just thought it was much, much more than it should be.

~

Shiners, in the minnow bucket, darted left and right. Night crawlers we filched by the light of night's moon tunneled dirt in the coffee can. Bait. "Live things to catch live things," Dad always said each time he slipped the thin hook through a slippery body, but I heard it different that day.

He cast. Set the pole in the wooden wye he carved from a cherry tree branch.

"Always use thin wire hooks and rig close to the tail so it can still move a lot. Or through the top of its back. You want it lively in the water. Just as it would be if it wasn't on the hook."

I nodded and straightened my back, rubbed at my spine. He glanced at me, then grabbed a minnow from the bucket and placed it in my palm.

"Hold on to that for a sec," he said. He pulled his lighter from his shirt pocket and relit the charred end of his cigarette. Took in a long drag. I watched the smoke come out his nose and thought of gills, of the insides of our lungs, and wondered if they were red, too. The minnow's tickle made my throat burn, made me want to clamp tighter, but I didn't want it dead. I blinked. I swallowed all that extra saliva. I thought about where he'd slip the hook through the one I held.

That's when he said, "Uncle Fatso takes them close to the eyeball and through the snout. They'll wiggle then." He laughed. "Here," he said. I opened my hand and watched its shine flip to the ground. "Son of a bitch," he said, stopping it with his boot from flip-flopping its way toward the water's edge. He grabbed it after two tries and handed it to me again. "Don't worry, you can use them like this, too. Hook straight through both lips. See?" I rolled my lips in while he slid the dead minnow on my line's hook. "Living or dead they still look good to the trout." He took in another drag and winked.

We moved to nightcrawlers then. We waited for a hit while the other worms burrowed deep to the bottom of the can, away from the light splashing through the trees that lined the bank. I couldn't help staring into the minnow bucket, watching their frantic flickers, their wild eyes.

～

Five bleeds later, I got hints when it would come on. Angry at my cowlick. Lonely. Fish looked sad. It scared me, this thing happening to me. Hurt all over. Made me slow. Run-down.

"Maybe flow's off a little," Dad said. "Maybe it'll straighten out." Though he told me that before Mom left us for Jesus and moved to a place in upstate New York to be nearer His Grace and Love, she'd had the exact same kind of pains. He wanted to take me to Crazy Miss Jean for a tincture, but I was so scared of her that I refused to go.

So, again, he took me fishing. We caught our limit quick. Let the gutted fish soak in salt water in the sink all day. After supper, Dad said, "Let's have a sundae." I couldn't bring myself to grab the maraschino cherry jar that always sat next to the salmon eggs after I spotted the canned plums. They looked too much like the clots that dropped from inside me.

"Hot fudge is plenty," I said.

In those five months, I'd learned to hate all things red.

That frightening leaking out came again just as I was half-way done with the sundae, sending the bowl clanging into the sink and me running to the bathroom. When I sat on the toilet, I imagined my own eggs sliding to the bottom of the porcelain while I peed.

"You okay?" Dad said from behind the bathroom door.

"I'm fine," I said, shoring up my voice box to keep at bay any sound of stupid crying.

≈

After eight bleeds, Dad told me to head out to the Sidle, wade in the water some. Might cure me from bleeding so much. But I worried the Sidle couldn't help me, and I didn't want to use the creek wrong like Miss Turner, didn't want to spook the fish away. He said, "Regular season's over. They've slowed by now."

≈

Cramps woke me. Cramps kept me home from school. Headaches weighted my eye sockets.

Snow came early. I tried to think about the cool creek water, how oxygen would be swelling, how trout hens would be building nests in the gravels, deep in the redds, to home their eggs.

≈

A year more had passed when Dad said, "I can't have you suffer," and went to Crazy Miss Jean without me. She said it was a malady no one aspired to study for a long time. She said she had it, too, 'til she went through the change. She said people still think it's fake, a lie. She told him what kinds of stones to find at the Sidle, gave him a bottle of paregoric and told him to mix it with sugar.

"It tastes like black licorice gone bad," he said and held the tiny whiskey glass to my lips. I forced myself to drink it.

Warm, warmer. Cramps eased, eyelids drooped. Rest came. Until pain rippled again.

Miss Jean told Dad to "search for a keen doctor who'll listen." She said it might take years. She gave the awful thing a name. "Endometriosis, endometriosis, endometriosis," Dad said.

I repeated it. It didn't sound half as mean as it was.

Dad said, "It's a dirty rotten shame."

In my floating self, I said, real quiet, "Will you help me build a wall, Dad, from both creek rock and river rock? It'll be knee-high and I'll plant flowers to line it."

"Sure will," he said.

From the steeped water in the pot, Dad took the smooth flat stones he found near the redds where the trout laid eggs. He placed the warm stones right on top of my belly where Miss Jean said my ovaries and uterus ached underneath. I could feel the Sidle's love walking deep inside. It made me want to live.

I stared at the rainbow Dad had mounted on my wall. I'd caught it on opening day near the bend where Lee cut the line on his palomino when he saw Granddad slump, where he held whiskey to Granddad's lip. The shininess, those pretty dots, that magenta line the length of it. Its colors buoyed me. It stared back at me with its hopeful eye.

Steer

Roy's truck almost stalled out as he slowed nearly to a stop passing the Blackwell farm, searching the field for the three calves he'd seen the day before. There they were, again, skipping, kicking, happy as could be. Roy smiled, but at the same time, his throat tightened up. That had been happening lately. Why? Hell, he didn't know. He grabbed a few gears, shifted his eyes back to the narrow road, careful not to sink a tire in the berm, and he thought about when they might tar and chip it, if they'd properly clear the ditch line first, put down a better base, crown the road. By the time he let himself look into the rearview to find the calves again, he was too far gone.

He was coming up on fifty; his only son would be sixteen in three months. Legs lengthened, voice deepened, chest broadened. Roy wanted nothing more than to teach him how to be a man who could handle what life threw. But he wanted him, also, to be free and light and open. He feared his son would inherit from him the maintenance and heft of this border around his heart he was constantly buttressing and closing off to guarantee hurt would not breach it.

"What am I even feeling?" he'd ask himself each day when anxiety nettled him, or worse, when it clamped off his air and made him dizzy. If he could only see where it started, its foundation, or find a crack, take a sledge to it, and bar it free.

He headed down Hogback Hill and something in the way the wipers trembled against the glass, the shimmying rattle of the truck and the growl of the retarder, the way the trees looked like they were whizzing past, tightened his throat in the worst way.

Through the dip, the truck took off. Halfway up the other side of the hill it creeped. Roy flicked on his four-ways.

He was relieved that his son hadn't seen all he had seen because he feared it would take him out. How to both ready him for and protect him from those things? Roy's father had only taught him to push through, avoid, ignore. Put out fires, work hard, dig deep, build fences and walls to man what you have.

As strong as he tried to be, creeping up hills in the truck, the roar of the motor when it geared down, especially the dashboard lit up with the intermittent flashing of the four-ways, never ceased to make him half sick in the stomach, half ready to bawl his eyes out. Most days he just breathed through it. Today was different. Today he let himself go the whole way back to when he was sixteen. Back to the steer.

∼

When Roy was his son's age, their steer found a gap in their fence. Got out. Somehow made it to the highway, crossed over. Likely chased down by traffic, it got itself turned around. Tiller Shanty, the neighbor down the way, called, said he'd roped it, no worry, had it there at his place tied up good.

When Roy and his dad made it to Tiller's place, they saw the steer fastened to an oak, just past a row of crab apples in full bloom. Roy took in a quick breath and grinned.

Roy's family lived just off the main route north to the mountains. Their backyard had become a small hobby farm to his father. They had laying chickens, a few goats, some guinea fowl to keep Lyme disease at bay, and this steer that Roy hadn't let loose. He had nothing in it. It just wanted to eat, got free of the fence and then lost. But somehow Roy's father had made him feel guilty, responsible for what had happened.

Of course, they couldn't load it in the pickup, but they could "walk it back." His dad tied the rope to the bumper of the truck. At first it did pretty good keeping up. Roy sat in the bed of the truck, watching it come along, watching it tugging at the rope every few seconds.

It was a Friday evening. Mountain traffic lined up behind their pickup as they made it almost to the top of the hill where they'd have to turn left off the highway and make the last leg home. Roy hoped the drivers wouldn't start their honking and scare the steer more. The pickup's four-ways blinked red in the steer's eyes.

Since Roy didn't have his driver's license yet he had to be the one in the back, the one to watch the steer come along. It was so tired now from all its running, and as he watched it he felt something like anger—toward what? The steer? His father? Himself? And he felt something else, too. Deep fear and panic. His eyes filled up with it and he could see it in the steer's eyes as well. Desperation, too, as he realized what was coming. In fact, he'd seen a glimpse of it as soon as his father snugged that rope to the bumper, saying, "Well, serves the damn thing right. It'll learn its lesson. Won't run off next time. It ran itself this far; it can run itself back." He'd seen it coming as soon as he realized the steer might not have the gumption in it to make it the whole way home.

When his father turned left off the highway, the steer wasn't ready for the turn and stumbled. The rope tugged at its neck and it swung its head left, right, up and down, to get free of it. Its front hooves folded under. It went down, onto its side, and his father dragged it the rest of the way. Roy wanted to turn away, put his head down, but he couldn't. He watched its body bounce, its head sliding against the road. He'd learned long ago how to calm the steer by rubbing its cheek and neck. He'd watched its ears come down in comfort. His grandfather taught him that. Its ears were not beagle dog-soft but coarse, filled with prickly hair. Still, he knew nothing could hold up to the asphalt's scrape. He was right. One ear had been ripped loose.

Roy heard his father's warning again in his head. But Roy knew the steer couldn't figure any of it out. It couldn't know cause and effect. Roy knew, as its body slid over the asphalt, all it felt was burning pain. All it wanted was to free itself from that rope. All it wanted was not to hurt.

Roy watched it lie there in the driveway on its side, panting, froth pushing out of its mouth and nostrils. Dark red blood rose up through the road dust on its coat. His father left him there and walked to the house to call Byler's meats from up over the hill.

He couldn't remember now the type of gun they used, or the men's faces, but he could still hear the shot. He could still see the wheels of the rendering truck, how the paint was chipping, how they were pitted with rust. He could still smell the diesel exhaust—his dad said, "They've a leak in their manifold." He could still see the light pink crab apple petals stuck to his tattered boots.

But Roy put that steer's heaving limp body, its eyes, the sound of its breath, deep into the muddy mortar around his heart and felt it stiffen and hold.

~

Now Roy couldn't seem to catch his breath. He pulled off onto the berm, sat still in the idling truck. He stared at the small map of gears on the stick and that line that was nothing but neutral.

He picked up the phone and dialed his wife. Said her name.

"You okay, Roy?" Her voice soothed him. That she could tell he might not be okay just by the way he said a few words comforted him.

"Yeah, sure," he said. "Hey, I meant to tell you, there's new little calves at the Blackwell farm. Cute little things."

"That right?"

"Yep. Cutest little things," he said again.

Seed to Full

*A*fter you've felled the tree and dragged it from the site and hauled it to the mill, one of the first things you do is scale it, measure to find out how many board feet it can yield.

Always measure the small end.

According to the Vermont Log Rule, a log with a diameter of eleven inches cut into a nine-foot length offers up about forty-five board feet. One that's thirty-six inches in diameter, same length, should yield 486 board feet.

Then you have to grade it.

Check for knots and branch stubs, seams with ingrown bark, ring shake, gum spots in black cherry.

I've started to teach our daughter, Myra, how to grade and scale, and she's shown promise. She has a head for numbers, for recall.

We've had this business for thirty-five years. My father sought out permission from the bishop to start up before I was born, and he's been milling every season since. Now I'm sawyer and he's more known for his work as a hammerman or saw smith, fixing our saws and those of nearby mills, Amish and English.

Myra's interest lies more in his job. By the time she was four, she knew the difference between a cross peen, a twist face, and a dog head. She knew how to measure blade tension and dishing when she was only eight. It comes natural to her. To right things. She doesn't even flinch when he pounds out the saws.

Then there's the saw kerf, the width of cut made by the saw. That loss has to be factored in, too. I can tell you exactly what each cut will do. I can tell you what type of cut is best for each kind of job: quartersawn, rift-sawn, flat-sawn. I can tell you the type of wood or how wet it is by the sound it makes when it meets the blade.

What I can't tell you is how much my wife Hannah's been hurt by how I've cut her or how wide the kerf is that I've laid upon her heart.

When you marry, scripture says you are joined together, but in truth, to do that you have to be cut away from your family, you cut away from yourself. These cuts are necessary.

But I've done more than that.

I've given her another seed that wouldn't grow.

∼

My wife Hannah's like a quartersawn board, the kind that's best for flooring or treads on stairs—it's stable, doesn't easily produce slivers or warp or cup, like flat-sawn wood. Flat-sawn's best only for visual appeal, like my eldest brother's wife. Rift-sawn's the worst cut of all, like my mother-in-law.

That's why it was so hard to take when Hannah slammed the screen door on me after I showed her the casket. I'd built it straight and true from wood I'd myself sanded and stained, rubbed with linseed until my hands were raw.

"*Too small*," she whispered. Only that.

But little Daniel fit into it easily, despite the thick blanket she'd wrapped him in. Perhaps she thought her love for him might somehow expand his small body, might help him to continue his growth, even underground.

"It's thirty-one-and-a-half by thirteen-and-a-quarter by eleven inches," I said, as if to convince her.

Myra stood at my side. Hannah just stared at us and shook her head, back and forth and back, again and again.

I used poplar, known for its straight grain, uniformity of texture, its light weight—though that never mattered, for when I carried what I'd made to the grave, my boy inside my box, I could barely find the strength.

I'd thought Hannah would be pleased.

She'd been the one to find the small stand of poplars near Sidle Creek. She used to go there and lie on the ground beside the creek, the swell of our son part of her silhouette, and twirl their tulip-shaped leaves round her second finger and search the tops of the trees to spot their blossoms.

But she didn't even touch the box. Turned her head when I told her it was cherry stain I'd used. She'd have none of it.

The Fractal Geometry of Grief

*H*ubert Ashe fell in love with the doe in August, four months after his wife passed.

He told no one about the deer until October when he called to inform his son, Will, he wouldn't be joining him for Thanksgiving. He wouldn't feel comfortable leaving the cabin and the deer behind. Who would put out apples? Who would sprinkle corn?

"Are you sure, Dad?"

"Yes, I'm sure." Hubert gazed at the laptop's screen, the trail cam photos. His doe. He traced the white band around her nose. Clicked to the next shot. Touched her throat's white patch.

"But I don't want you to be alone, Dad."

"I'm fine," Hubert said. It was Will who was alone. Still single, in his late forties, he'd stumbled through relationships, never having unearthed a love that would sustain him.

Hubert closed the trail cam file. Home screen appeared. Genevieve's seventy-third birthday. Two days before Easter. Their last holiday together, posing in front of the redbud's shocking pink blossoms. Hubert's wide grin, disheveled hair, glasses crooked on his crooked nose. Will beaming, so tall, between them. Genevieve with her new white silk scarf tied at her throat, nearly matching the snow-white her once ginger hair had become. Her hand clutching a leaf. She was gone by the time the pink blossoms wilted and green heart-shaped leaves dressed that tree.

Hubert adjusted the phone at his ear. Will talked of flights and restaurants and day trips he'd planned for them. "Yes. Yes," Hubert said. He opened the construction file. He wanted the new glass room he'd designed for the doe to be a surprise for his son. It was almost complete. "Listen," Hubert said, "why don't you just come here? I'd love to have you, and you could meet her."

"Meet who?"

Hubert pulled the drapes aside. Was she in the yard yet? The building crew had put up barriers to keep all wildlife off the poured floor as it cured, but he knew she'd be curious. "My doe," he said.

Will laughed. "Well, listen, I'll just have to meet your doe at Christmas, because really, Dad, that's why I was hoping you could get *here*. There's no way I'll be able to get away over Thanksgiving with work and stuff."

"Okay, Professor! Get that semester buttoned up and I'll see you soon enough."

"Sounds good. Love you."

"Love you, too."

Hubert closed his laptop, stood next to the window searching the tree line for her. Outside he swept away the debris mud wasps had left on the battens, straightened his wood stack, the pine cone wreath on the door.

Miles McIntyre, Hubert's closest neighbor, came down the drive.

"Your boy wanted me to check, make sure you don't need anything," Miles said. He stood in the middle of the yard, his hulking frame squeezed into his weathered game warden's jacket, taking in the edges of the wooded lot, smoothing his beard and likely surveying the downed branches, the fallen black walnut's trunk Hubert hadn't gotten to yet. Maybe he was just remembering how much Genevieve, unlike Hubert, had loved collecting kindling, downed wood, or maybe he was remembering how she'd said, "I loathe their deaths but I do love how their loss opens up the canopy for others to grow, grow, grow." Hubert hadn't joined them last fall. He'd stayed on the porch out of their way.

"He must have called you as soon as we hung up. Well, you can tell Will I'm just fine, Miles," Hubert said. There wasn't any movement in the trees.

"Will do," Miles said, stepping from the porch.

"Yes, I am just fine," Hubert muttered, rubbing at his brow. But he wasn't. Two whitetail he'd noted in several trail cam captures hadn't appeared in three days: the twelve-point, part of a pre-rut bachelor group of four, and the little button buck that always grazed with Hubert's doe. Simply disappeared. Hubert knew from the pamphlet Miles had given him a month before that archery season was in, so he straightened up his shoulders, tried to sound perfectly calm as he asked, "Did anyone around here tag a twelve-point?" He steeled himself for the answer. It had been Miles who'd warned him not to get too attached to the wildlife when he'd first expressed his desire to handfeed the herd. "You're only asking for trouble. They'll want in your house." Still Miles had explained the steps of earning trust, which foods to use, how to talk, walk, move around them. Of course, Miles didn't know Hubert had fallen in love with one.

"Yep. Riley Bowser, Harold's grandson, got a nice one. You've met Harold, right? Yeah, big twelve-point. Lung shot. Quick." Hubert felt like air was being sucked from his lungs through some hole. "Put his picture in the paper, they did."

"And any little button bucks?" Hubert couldn't bear hearing it had been shot, but he had to know. It always looked so skittish in the photos. So wary. Just like him. He was informed. He wasn't naïve. He'd read the game commission's harvest report Miles had given him, knew the numbers. Thousands killed each season, antlered and antlerless.

"Not sure about a button buck," Miles said, kicking at the dried mud on his tires. "I'll ask around. Usually, archers go for the big racks, though. You sure you don't need anything?"

"I'm sure." Far off, the train from Echo to Brinie Furnace blew its crossing whistle, and high above a gray squirrel darted from one tall oak to another, sending acorns thudding to the ground.

"You okay, Hube?"

Hubert wiped his eyes with his handkerchief. This worry and crying would sometimes bubble up out of him with no warning. "Yes. These allergies. Molds. I think tree molds. They're worse this fall, worse than I remember them from last."

"Well, wet and hot summer. That's what we get, I guess."

"Yes, yes, it was." Hubert blew his nose. "Oh, you mentioned before you could post safety zone signs, right? I think one of those Ramers has been walking through here."

Miles took off his hat, pushed back his thinning hair, snugged it back on. "I don't think you'll have a problem, but, yeah, I can put some up later today."

"I'd appreciate that."

"Well, I gotta take off. Just call if you need anything, okay? And if you want help clearing the floor of these branches and such, say the word. Just got my saw sharpened."

"I sure will. Thank you kindly, Miles."

Miles saluted, a habit from when he was a Marine. He stopped. "You said the room's gonna be all glass, huh? When are they putting up the walls?"

"They said they'd start first thing Monday."

"It'll go pretty quick from there."

"I hope so," Hubert said, fingering one of the cardboard boxes that held the glass wall panels. They'd been sitting on the porch since delivery a few days before. He was so anxious to have the room completed. Now even more so since hunting season had begun.

As soon as Miles left, Hubert rushed to the house, to his computer. The local paper showed the smiling boy posing with the dead twelve-point, arrow threaded through its antlers, bow on the ground near one front hoof, quiver against its side, the boy's gloved hands grasping the rack. Hubert closed his eyes. Breathe. Don't get worked up. He had a porch to winterize. A shed to organize. Feed to scatter. He blew his nose again, shut his laptop.

His doe must have sensed his worry, much as he tried to push it away, for there she was by the shed waiting for him. Instead of slowly making his path to her, talking quietly, bridging the distance between them in a measured way, lest she leap and run, he yelled out, "You *must* stay close to the house. As close as you can." Her ear twitched. She turned to look behind the shed, and he ran to her. But she was like light itself, flying through the woods dodging saplings, stumps. A good fifty yards from him she stopped, turned around to look back, her markings slightly distinct from the last of the leaves.

"I'm sorry," he shouted. "I, I didn't mean to frighten you but I'm just so scared something is going to, to happen. Please just stay as close as you can." She hesitated for a moment, then meandered farther and farther, camouflaged now completely by the trees. His eyes searched. Again, he thought of running to her, but he didn't want to frighten her more. He didn't want to tell her how his mind traveled to such horrible places where he pictured her zigzagged rush from the pain of a bullet or imagined her dropped in the berm, hit by a reckless driver, or found her bedded down in her favorite spot near Sidle Creek, but bleeding from multiple wounds, a spray of the shotgun—some pellets unable to penetrate her hide, others finding her heart and lungs and belly.

Movement. No. Not her. How he wished for a glimpse of her late summer coat, that ginger tone it had been when he'd first met her. But now her coat had changed to the color of wintered trees, a blueish tan that fall weather and a needed cover for survival had made her.

There. There she was now. He squinted. There. Blending completely but for the white rings around her eyes and muzzle.

And then, gone again.

He bit his lip as he struggled to remove the thick plastic from the mineral block. He carried it to the small stand, his head thumping to its edges with dread. He dipped the coffee can into the large bag of shucked corn. Sprinkled the yellow around the mineral block. He waited outside the shed for over an hour for her return, but not one deer came in to feed.

～

Hubert and Genevieve moved to her family land in rural western Pennsylvania forty miles north of Pittsburgh, almost three years before. Far, both mentally and physically, from their former university positions, it was a secluded nine-acre lot isolated from everything domestic and human. Filled with everything feral, wild. The cabin itself was a small saltbox built by Genevieve's great-grandfather, and they'd both agreed—Hubert somewhat reticently, she most insistently—that they live there once they both retired. "Can't let it sit empty any longer, Hube," she had said year after year when he kept putting off the move. "My math is in the city" was his mantra, to which Genevieve would counter, "You know math is everywhere. It will be in the woods, too. You'll see."

Hubert was a mathematician, a finalist for the Fields Medal, whose special areas of study were statistical mechanics and geometry. Genevieve was an animal behaviorist and part-time consultant for the zoo, but most of her research took place in the bright hum of the lab's fluorescence. "I need the trees, the leaves, the forest floor," she'd often say as she stood looking out the windows of her lab in the direction of Schenley Park where she'd walk each day, begging Hubert to join her. He never did.

He'd dwell in his cluttered office where he'd find Genevieve's doodles of gingko leaves and acorns on his tablet notes, on his chalkboard and whiteboard, and then at home on the large bedroom windows where he'd sometimes sketch out theorems with his grease pencils if the math visited him in a dream.

They arrived at the cabin in the summertime when all the wood surrounding it was heavy with green, thick with the scent of bark expanding. The wildlife hid from view but called well into the night and in the earliest hints of morning. "Annoying," Hubert called the late evening din of what he would eventually learn was frog song.

"I think they're lovely, these jazzy tunes and bluesy melodies," Genevieve replied and leaned in to kiss Hubert. "Perfect pitch, perfect harmony, don't you think?"

In the time they'd lived there together, Hubert had taken only one walk beyond the manicured landscaped acre surrounding the cabin. He was afraid he'd contract poison ivy; he had a fanatical fear of ticks and snakes; he worried he'd twist an ankle in a hole of some kind. She'd tried teasing him into the dark haunt of it at night to help her track the deer, those animals she was most obsessed with, but he waited on the porch, hearing her rustling and moving alone.

So, when his hands would reach for her—in those weeks after everyone had long walked away from him standing, staring at her casket, those living wives of his friends sinking heels into sod, navigated by their husbands to cars, to closed doors, to car engines starting and gravel popping—in those days when he needed just to feel her slender wrists, he wandered through the woods, tripping over brambles, kicking through brush. He needed to touch something growing. What did he care if he stepped into some hole that would sink him? What did he need to do to *feel* again?

Then one morning, in late spring's business of green and growth, Hubert started to count things. It helped. That day he counted fifteen hemlocks on the east side of the lot. Seven hickories. He used Genevieve's tree identification booklet, flipping pages, considering bark, edges of leaves, alternate and opposite branching, and he choked up when he saw her annotations in the back—her handwriting making her somehow present again. He scratched out the words, immediately regretting it, collapsing at the base of an oak, crying.

In those days, anything could upend him: a stray cat's fur left behind on the porch cushions, a mud wasp's whining, a bird splashing in a puddle after a rainstorm. All things Genevieve would have pointed out had she still been with him. However, in counting he seemed to find center, so for weeks he continued to count random things to pilot his days—ratios of pine squirrels to gray squirrels, ashes to oaks, cirrus fibrates to cirrus duplicatus, lobed leaves to spiked. It wasn't that he was trying to order things, exactly; it wasn't that he didn't understand the randomness of her death. Perhaps he understood far too well the patterns that randomness offered. He counted finite things—mayapple plants one day, thistles the next. But he became exhausted when the number reached triple digits and perplexed by his own counting grid.

Memories of Genevieve's touch stunned him always. Once she had rubbed leaves of some helpful plant to the reddened undersides of his forearms. He railed against himself for losing the name of the plant, for forgetting what it had looked like. "The same woods give us the culprit and the antidote. Stop your scratching, Hube." He couldn't help it. He recalled with profound, endless regret that he had pushed her hands away, scratched until his arms were hot, his skin broken and weeping, as if his skin, then, already knew the loss of her touch. His whole mind, as he grieved, suffered the sensation of something underneath that needed scratching, needed touching. In these moments, it was best to keep going back to his numbers. He redrew the grid on his pad. Lifted the strings from the edge of the quadrant patch of mayapple. Started over again.

But night would come. Sleep would not. Endless insomnia. Endless pain. And guilt. What had he missed? Could he have prevented the inevitable somehow?

The night she died she was a bit tired. Went to bed early. "Just some indigestion," she'd whispered as she kissed him goodnight. He vaguely remembered her patting her belly. When he awoke several hours later, she was cool, cold, gone.

He turned first to mathematics to try to figure it out.

He knew it was his ongoing research that kept him from obsessing about the signs he saw early on after their move that made him believe his wife's heart would soon stop. He'd questioned her, but she explained away her exhaustion. "Hube, my body is simply besieged by the sensory details of the trees." She said her jaw pain was from constant smiling and trying to whistle like the birds.

He knew what made her die. He had looked closely at the statistics of heart attacks in women Genevieve's age, by computing her extensive profile, lifestyle, family history, levels of cholesterol, all of the data the doctor's and pathologist's reports offered.

He did not know why she was gone.

~

Miles returned at daybreak the very next day and posted several safety zone signs around the perimeter. "You're in good shape now, but I don't think you have anything to worry about."

"Well, thank you just the same," Hubert said. "I'm off to check my trail cams." He'd seen what he'd thought was the shadow of a man in one shot from the cameras, figured it might be one of the Ramers following a flock of turkey. Or was he being paranoid?

"Seeing anything exciting?" Miles asked. "Most I've seen is one gobbler—one single gobbler." He spat, hitched up his pants. "Oh, and I'm getting great shots of all the raccoon and possum a soul would ever want. That's all that wants to visit with me." He laughed his jolly laugh, climbed into his cab.

Hubert said, "I meant to tell you I ordered one of those no-glow infrareds you suggested."

"Get yourself a white flash. It spooks them a little, but the quality is amazing."

"I'll think about that," Hubert said. He had thought about it. He didn't want to harm his doe's eyes.

He wandered along the foot trails his constant checks had worn, surveying the lot, emptying each camera. He climbed up into the old tree stand a neighbor had used to hunt years before. There, his doe. A close-up in his binoculars. She stood exactly where she always was this time of day, way off in the neighboring field. He blew out a breath of relief as he rotated the diopter and her image came clearer. Perfect. Her movements so graceful, smooth. He tried to keep his hands from their trembling, resting his elbows on the post meant at one time to steady a gun's barrel. He shunted that thought away.

She leisured through the corn stubble, her silhouette in relief against the last standing stalks. Far beyond, Miles's red barn roof.

In the other direction, the slice through the woods where the train track curved.

Back in the field, she was gone.

He fiddled with the fly wheel and the dead corn stalks came into focus. Not her. He scanned from one corner of the field to the other. Nothing. His glasses fogged, so he quickly wiped them on the tail of his shirt, settled them back against his face, readjusted the binoculars. He took in a deep breath, waiting a few more minutes to see if she would reemerge at the woods line.

She didn't.

So he climbed down, headed back to the cabin.

Maybe she'd be in the yard when he returned.

As he rounded the last section of his trail, something shined in the dropped leaves. An empty beer can partly covered, smashed thin and dirtied with what looked like woods dirt, or road grime. Had an animal dragged it here? Did someone leave it behind? He fell to his knees, spread his hands along the pine needles looking for—what? A cigarette butt? A boot print?

Miles had assured Hubert and Genevieve that hunters knew their lot was off-limits. Not long after they moved in, Miles had given Genevieve an old flame-orange vest with a PA Game Commission patch on it, and he told her, "I did what you asked. I put the word out to your neighbors, the Ramers and Thompsons. I said you hike daily and we don't need accidents. There's plenty of good hunting away from your piece here."

Genevieve said, "I'll still wear this, just in case." And she did.

Miles said, "You're too pretty to mistake for a deer or a bear or anything but a beauty queen." Genevieve snorted, hugged him.

Hubert had watched from the balcony, wanting to join her, yearning to be venturesome.

Now he sniffed at the can, but there was no lingering scent

of beer. He studied the scratches, the color, trying to imagine how long it had been there. Was it faded from the sun? He wasn't familiar with this brand. Some microbrew. He ran to the cabin, tripping over brambles tearing at his ankles.

At the computer he downloaded the trail cams' photo cards. Maybe he'd see who'd been walking there. His ankles were itchy. Thorns. Stuck in his socks. His ankles weeping blood. "Damn it!" he yelled. "Damn it, damn it, damn it!"

In the laundry room he found the first aid kit Genevieve kept stocked.

"Soap and water is the best. Keep wounds clean and dry." Her voice still clear in his head. For this he was grateful.

When he returned to the computer, the photos had loaded and he saw his doe again. "Oh, there you are," he said. So many shots of her. Again and again. And no hunters, thank goodness. Just her. Her nose close to the mineral block. Bedding down in the pine needles. A blur here and there, her eyes glowing from the flash. He'd have to replace those cameras. In some shots she was perfectly focused, her hide so close to the lens that the tufts looked as though they could be touched. In the early morning shots with sun flitting through the trees, her tender eyes looked straight into the camera's lens, into Hubert's eyes, into his cracked heart.

He ran through the dozens of shots again, deleting empty ones, moving each photo of his doe to her own file. When he was through, he rubbed his forehead, dropped his shoulders. "How tense you are, Hube. Relax. You've been at this too long." Genevieve would always pull him away from his notes, his computer, and beg him to take a walk. He could almost feel her hands on his shoulders now, kneading the knots away.

He entered the data into his spreadsheet that listed group size, when his doe traveled with fawns, yearlings, bucks, when she moved alone, and how close and often she came to the cabin. As usual, the longest strings of photos were at dusk but also around three a.m. The time, according to the coroner, Genevieve passed.

~

She died from an acute myocardial infarction. Left anterior descending artery. He'd been sleeping beside her as the blockage halted her heart, as the muscle died, as her respirations sped up, slowed, then ultimately ceased.

"It was fast, Mr. Ashe. She didn't suffer," the coroner had said, shaking Hubert's hand.

Hubert had tried to rub away the stinging in his throat that commenced upon finding her when he'd called his son to inform him of Genevieve's passing. Will answered the phone so upbeat, gleeful, likely thinking Hubert was calling to wish him a Happy Birthday, maybe congratulate him on his promotion. Instead, his poor son had to navigate the awful silent gaps between Hubert's repetitive words, "She's gone."

Will said, a week after the funeral when he packed to leave, "You couldn't have saved her. Don't beat yourself up like this. You know you can stay with me if you change your mind. Promise me you won't sit around worrying about what you might have done differently. The cardiologist made it clear, too, okay?"

Hubert had promised Will that day that he would be fine. But he couldn't help it; he raged at himself daily for all the things he might have done differently, for all the time lost to them when she died. Bitterness took over his mind. And where bitterness didn't take hold, anger did.

And he lost his mind along with losing Genevieve. He couldn't concentrate enough to read anything. Even his own articles were filled with foreign words.

But counting and identifying the trees seemed to steady the bitterness, the rage. Maybe it was because Genevieve had made it her mission to know them. So he would, too. He found calm walking through the mixed-age timber stands surrounding the cabin with Genevieve's guide for deciduous trees of the northeast. Like her, he always returned from his long walks with fans of leaves in both hands. Like her, he'd spread them out on the kitchen table.

"Find a new one?" he'd always say, watching her wrinkle her brow at the shape of the leaf, look away out the window and then closely at the leaf again.

One day she said, "They're all new. Each year they become"— she stopped, looked at him, and smoothed the hair back on his forehead—"new trees."

On one of her last days, she'd said, "You know, I think we have over twenty species here." She scratched the name of a tree on the list she had posted on the side of the refrigerator. She placed each of five leaves between pages of Hubert's books. "Another oak fell." She had been preoccupied by their strength but also their sudden deaths. "When they fall, they leave such a large hole." Why hadn't he hugged her when she'd said that?

He regretted never understanding how deeply she loved the trees. Once she'd said, "I could see them all the time if we just knocked out these walls and installed more windows. Floor to ceiling! Let's do it, Hube! A whole glass house!" He watched her move to the counter to lift a tea towel from the muffins—apple and walnut, still warm.

If only he could go back.

When she'd heard a neighbor up the road was clear-cutting his timber stands, she wept with disgust.

When she found the rub a velvet-antlered buck had made, she wept with awe.

"We are all connected to the trees, Hube!" she had said, more than once.

Walking among them, touching the spots she likely touched, made him feel closer to her. So it didn't surprise him when he was mixed up in the trees that he encountered his first deer in person. A fawn.

He'd just pulled a small limb down to investigate its properties, his wedding band loose, cool on his finger. He hadn't been eating full meals since all of the containers Will left in his freezer were gone. He moved the band back over the soft folds of his knuckle. On the limb, he noted the texture, the small knots of growth. It might be a river birch? He checked the ridges and undersides of leaves. Were they opposite or alternate? He flipped pages, followed simplified icons. "Symmetric? Asymmetric?" he said with each inspection. More pages, more leaves. His words slipped into the bark, into the dirt below, hopefully finding hers.

Birch. Yes. As he was gently tearing a filmy layer of bark, there was a blur of something to the right of him. He was caught by the spots of a fawn skirting the edge of the woods. He stood, shaded his eyes from the sun that followed it too, spotted, through the trees. His legs numbed. He steadied himself, his back to the trunk of the small birch, and slowly let out his breath to keep from startling it. He had been noting eating patterns of all animals by the hints they would leave behind: the broken branches, trodden soil near berry bushes, the white milky weep on chewed stalks of perennials. This fawn was content enough to pass the shrubs and flowers that spread their sweet vulnerability to woodland animals. It was still being nursed.

He wanted to follow it but knew he shouldn't. When he stepped away from the tree the fawn raised its head.

Looked to the woods.

Looked back at Hubert.

Back to the woods.

It let out a high-pitched bleat, took off.

Hope clamped Hubert's heart like a red-tailed hawk, its talons embedded deep in the muscle, knifing a wonderful pain to his chest that made tears finally, finally, come. He cried and laughed and let out the breath he'd been holding since Genevieve passed.

But it was later that night that real hope and promise and love made its way to him.

After seeing this fawn, he was more like his old self and decided to read again. Numbers had stayed with him, but words, those sly messengers of feeling and memory, those envoys of both understanding and bewilderment, had kept themselves hidden. He settled himself on the porch with a glass of wine, some of his old notes, and a favorite book Genevieve had given him one Christmas, Benoit Mandelbrot's *The Fractal Geometry of Nature.*

And that's when she came into the yard.

There was something in the way she lingered, knowing he was there, that made him offer a simple, "Hello." She didn't run away. So he continued, "I'm Hubert."

She looked up with what seemed to him poised inquisitiveness. First she looked at his eyes, then down to the ground, dipping her head, then looked back up, tail twitching.

"I'm reading, well, a book . . . on . . . mathematics. Specifically, fractals." He smiled at his own words floating there with the hawk call and leaf drop.

She looked behind her, dipping her head again, moved a few steps, not away. "What would your name be?"

The sound of a branch snapping set her off, leaping three leaps and seemingly gone. But several yards away, she stood, half hidden by a tree. She looked back. Moved slowly, hesitantly, from him and his smile, his squinting to see her.

He continued reading, aloud this time, about Fermat's spiral. "As in sunflowers," he said, nodding at her. "And there are fern fractals," he said, reading on, and she listened, dipping her head. "There is this way of looking at nature, mathematically."

She stood still for several minutes, and then was gone.

All through the night he pulled book after book off his shelves and read. Not just his own mathematics texts but books Genevieve had recommended. These uncovered more about another kind of woods he'd never completely considered—about how the plants and animals of the forest imparted hints to humans about the land, the weather, and the subtle changes in the earth, life, decay, and death, glimpses of infinity. Leaves Genevieve had collected, pressed in these books, fell out as he turned the pages and tears spilled from his eyes. Even so, he read more, falling asleep with his glasses still on. When he woke, he went straight to the balcony and there she was again, dipping her head, milling at the edges of the yard, feasting on the rhododendron's magenta flowers. The wood's hum hushed with the covering of dew. He tapped a knuckle on the banister. "I'll be darned. Is it you?" She looked straight at him.

~

Hubert stood at the rhododendrons now. Waiting. It was dusk and he was still concerned about who had left the beer can behind. Maybe they were not just wandering, but scouting, looking for scrapes and rubs. Maybe a hunter from another county, state?

Just then, gunshots rang out, seeming to come from the fields to the west. Hubert stood still, baffled. Waiting. More shots. Rapid-fire.

He immediately called Miles.

"Shooting rifles, is all," Miles said.

"Target shooting?"

"Yeah, that's it. They like to break their guns in well before first day."

"Oh. I see."

Hubert sat at the table holding the phone long after his call with Miles ended.

Finally, he jumped up and gathered his flashlight, matches, newspaper, a small hatchet, and his sleeping bag. He loaded some dry wood into a burlap sack and made his way into the trees. He located the spot in the woods near where his doe bedded down and spread out his sleeping bag next to his small pile of wood and kindling.

The fire kept going out. The wood was damper than he thought.

He fell asleep for a few hours but she never came in.

At dawn he was startled awake by Miles's voice. "You'll catch your death, Hube!" Miles helped him stand and wrapped the sleeping bag around him.

"I'm fine. I can walk," Hubert said as Miles started to lift him. They trudged back, their breath breaking into little clouds that melded between them.

"It got down to frost last night. Look." Miles nodded to the yard, a muted shade of green. "You've gotta dress for the weather, man. What were you doing? I saw the smoke from my place and came right away."

"Oh, just thought I'd see what it's like to be out all night. Didn't mean to cause you alarm."

He wanted to tell him. When Hubert had once confided that waking to find his doe at the edge of the woods filled him with "measureless adoration," Miles had said, "Now you see why I do this work. Nature is perfect." But Miles couldn't grasp how deeply Hubert's affection ran. Miles knew the habits and habitats of deer, but had he tasted the same woody branches they tasted?

"No trouble at all," Miles said. "But are you okay?"

"I'm fine. I'm so sorry."

"No apologies. Now you should get warmed up, take a hot shower. You need me to stay and make you something to eat? It's no trouble."

"No, no. You've done enough already. I'm just fine."

"Okay, then. You sure, though?" Miles smoothed his beard.

Hubert made a joke about probably being too old for camping out. "Really, I'm just fine," he said again and again until Miles seemed convinced and left.

But he wasn't fine. He made several calls to his contractor, finally connecting with him and inquiring about the timeline and how quickly they could finish up. If he had one carpenter's bone in his body, he would have installed the walls himself. But he had to wait. All day Sunday he paced his house, the yard, the concrete slab where the glass room would be erected. His doe stayed at the edge of the yard and didn't even come in to feed from his hand. He'd upset her with his panic but he couldn't help himself.

Monday morning Miles was there to watch the construction. "Sunlight's good for the bones. Vitamin D!" Miles said as the men set the bulletproof panels into place.

"Yes." Hubert tried to smile but he was gripped by a fear he couldn't begin to make Miles understand.

Later, after Miles and the crew left, the doe came back, sauntered along the tree line, and then approached the room. "This will keep you safe," Hubert said, knocking on the glass. He spread corn kernels on the tree stump between them. She came in close to sniff and then moved back. "It's okay," he said, spreading more kernels on the surface.

Each day she moved in closer. By the end of the week, she almost walked into the room.

"I'll keep it heated by small convection heaters, slim panels, four hundred watts each."

She dipped her head, lifted it quickly.

"The contractor suggested I check into a solar panel they could install on the roof of the main house." She came in closer, ate from his palm as he stood in the threshold chatting away. He was shocked, shaking with delight. How warm her breath on his palm. Her eyes fixed on his. But she didn't come in.

The next evening, after the crew left, he brought slices of peach out to the room.

"It's nearly complete," he said as she darted in close to take a piece, then darted away, back, away. He giggled. He said, "I love you."

She didn't answer, but he knew how she felt.

The next day the room was complete. "Looks nice," Miles said. Hubert nodded, nearly moved to tears, preoccupied by what he'd *not* seen on the trail cameras. Another two deer in the regular herd of six—a spike and a doe—had disappeared.

"Bucks in full rut right now," Miles said to the crew as they packed up. "Watch driving out of here."

Hubert busied himself by lining his favorite books on low shelves. The first evening he slept in the glass room, he read Dickinson from Genevieve's journal: "A wounded deer leaps highest, I've heard the hunter tell." A pine squirrel darted up the edge of the room, stopped, looked in.

"But there will be no wounded deer now," Hubert said, seeing his reflection in the glass. There, near the back edge of the yard, stood his doe. Slowly she came to the walkway, slowly to the room.

Hubert opened the French doors and called her in but she stayed outside, sniffing the gravel edging around the perimeter. "There's plenty of space," he said. But even the apples and peaches couldn't convince her to come over the threshold.

Finally, Thanksgiving evening, after Hubert talked to Will on the phone while eating some of the leftovers Miles dropped off on his way home, he went to the glass room to try again. The opening of rifle season was just days away and he couldn't bear to think of her in the woods when hunters put on their first drives.

There was a light rain. Droplets on the glass sparkled.

He waited for her to appear at dusk as she often did, but she was nowhere in sight.

He turned on their old CD player, slid in the disc Will had made for Genevieve—her favorite songs. Tom Petty's "Walls," began to play while he carefully spread the sliced peaches on a platter near the entrance. He closed his eyes, listening, hoping. But when he opened them, still she wasn't there.

He stood at the entrance, tapping his finger on the jamb, when all at once shots rang out, echoing through the valley. It was nearly dark. Hubert ran to the house, dialed Miles's number.

"Did you hear shots? Why are people shooting at this hour? It's too dark to hit a target. There were five shots from up near Ramer's place. Near the field. Did you hear?"

"I did. I'll go check it out. You're right. It's not safe. I'll check."

Hubert returned to the glass room and paced.

When he heard nothing from Miles, he called again and again, leaving several messages. A rain-snow mix started, landing and melting on the glass.

Finally, Miles came. "Hube. I got your messages. Couldn't make out what you were saying."

"I was trying to explain, I—"

"Hube, are you okay?"

"I think those shots were for her."

"Who?"

"My love, my—"

"Who?"

"My doe."

"Hey, okay, now calm down." Miles handed Hubert his handkerchief. "Here."

Hubert took it and wiped his eyes. He told him how he'd tried to get her to come into the room, and he watched Miles's face contort with each word. "What? Say something, Miles."

"Hube, the Ramers may have shot her. I'm so sorry. They have red tags."

"What are you talking about?"

"Red tags allow farmers to hunt deer out of season if they feel they're causing damage. But the Ramers have no business on your land and you can be sure I'll fine them for that if they were, but by law they are allowed to bag as many deer as necess—"

"Take me to her." Hubert couldn't stop shaking.

"What?" Miles asked.

"I want to see her. If they shot her, I want to see her."

"Okay, okay, I can do that."

Sleet hit the windshield and Miles mumbled about black ice, about studded tires, about so many things on which Hubert could not focus. He only saw his doe's eyes staring into his. The way she hesitated at the threshold of the glass room.

They pulled into the Ramer farm's long limestone drive. Wind lashed. Sleet blew sideways. "I'll come around and help you out," Miles said. "I don't want you slipping on the walk." Hubert waited for Miles to jog around the front of the truck, his collar up, his gloved hands covering his face from the weather.

Hubert braced as he walked through the barn doors. He covered his mouth and grabbed Miles's arm when he saw three deer hung there upside down, their back legs attached to the gambrel hoists on the rafters, carcasses split open, bleeding out onto the dusty straw-covered barn floor.

"What can I do ya for, gentlemen?" Butch Ramer asked, then

spat a long trail of tobacco juice onto the floor. In his hand he held a knife, a sharpening stone. Hubert felt a pain cut through his chest as he looked not up at the deer—he couldn't bear to look yet for her specific markings—but at the rafters above, at the lights, at the way the dust floated around swirling in some pattern he could not follow. His knees hit the floor. If not for Miles's quick hands he would have surely hit his head.

"Shit. Shit. Get a chair, or no, get something for him to lie on. You all right, sir?"

Hubert tried to focus on Butch Ramer's face, then on Miles's, but he could only see the three does swaying above and behind them. Hubert closed his eyes again. He could hear the men's hushed words.

He made himself open his eyes again and look. None of the deer seemed to have that scar on its neck like his doe. He tried to get up to see their faces more closely, markings around their eyes. He'd know if he could get closer.

"Whoa there. Just stay here for a minute 'til you get your bearings," Butch said.

They held him there. A man who looked like the younger Ramer he'd seen often at the Agway offered Hubert a sip of water from a mug. He took it and tried to thank him. He focused on Miles's eyes and words that seemed so foreign and distant. Miles's nervous tone. "Seems he's taken a liking to one from the herd that sticks close to his cabin," Miles said and pursed his lips. The others looked confused, eyes wide, shifting feet, but understanding, nodding, trying to smile at Hubert.

Finally, they helped him up to a sitting position. Hubert felt like he might pass out again but he had to be sure. He said, "The middle one. See her scar. Please get her down from there, please?"

The young Ramer looked to his father, who nodded back to him. "Yeah, ah, sure."

Hubert heard the whining pulley and nearly blacked out again.

"We don't have to do this right now," Miles said. "I can just take you back, okay?"

Hubert shook his head.

The three men placed the doe on the floor next to him.

It was her.

He slid himself closer, cradled her head in his arms, weeping. The scent of the woods, the leaves, the ferns and bark and grass and tiny bits of dirt he always smelled when he was near her. The scar on her neck that she never let him touch. Now he floated his fingers over it. Her delicate eyelashes, the markings of her muzzle he never kissed, and now he did. He couldn't help himself from wailing, from burying his face into her hide. He resisted their hands when they tried to separate him from his doe. He even kicked them away, burying his face in her neck again, saying, "I'm so so sorry, my love."

Miles got down beside Hubert, whispered, "Let me get you home, Hube, okay?" Hubert shook his head at first but then let Miles help him up from the floor and walk him to the truck. Miles talked the whole way back about nothing Hubert would remember; he called Will and said he was going to just stay over until Will came. He padded back down the hallway and checked on Hubert nearly every two hours, asking the same questions, saying the same words. "You okay? I didn't know, Hube. I mean, I didn't understand. I should have warned you about, well, getting close, you know. I'm so sorry, Hube."

Will drove the ten hours straight through from Vermont. Arrived late morning. They all met in the glass room. Miles shook Will's hand and Hubert hugged his son tight.

"Dad, I'm sorry. I just—I'm sorry. I didn't know."

Hubert didn't say a word, just pointed to the photos he'd taken—close-ups of ferns, sunflowers, pine cones. He turned to the close-ups of tree trunks, said, "See the tessellations in this bark, the pattern?"

His son pursed his lips. He said, "Yeah."

"Well, some has patterning easier to see. Some isn't there. But it's still beautiful. See? Oak, cherry, birch." He'd certainly make sure to tell his Will about the many flowers whose petals he'd counted and found Fibonacci numbers, 34, 55, 89. Not always, but the numbers hit enough to show his love for math and Genevieve's love for plants and trees was married. He flipped back and traced the curled lines of the sunflower's center. "See these patterns, the way the seeds grow. The same, this curve. The patterns. Everywhere. The Golden Ratio! Look at this one." He pointed to another picture where his son was sure to see it. "Your mother was right. Math is right here. She's right. Right here. She's still showing me. And here, here she is." He flipped through the dozens of photos of his doe taken by the infrared light of the trail cam and then by the light of the morning and evening sun. "Isn't she just beautiful?"

"Why don't you come stay with me for a while?" Will said. "You know winter's nice on the lake." Hubert flipped through the pages again, holding the book up every so often so Miles could see. "I know you miss Mom. Dad, listen, I'll help you pack some clothes. My spare room's all ready for you."

Miles nodded to Hubert.

Will closed the book. "Dad, you need to get away from here for a little while. Okay?"

Hubert moved his hand to his son's cheek, held it there. How could he explain that he couldn't leave now? This is where Genevieve would come back to him again. Not as a doe next time, but in some other way.

Sun glanced across the east side of the glass room. A small sapling, newly planted near the entrance, bent with the weight of a wren on its bough. The dusting of snow the night before had somehow brought a deep green back to the grass. Small mounds of snow, not yet melted away by the sun, dotted the lawn. Hubert stood and set the book on the small table. He looked through the glass to the oaks, birches, sycamores, maples, and deeper to the elms, ashes, hickories, quaking aspens, the tulip poplars. In time, he'd teach his son how to tell them apart. Now he needed to place himself between them and smell them and touch them.

Hubert walked from the room and into the woods, the deep, mysterious, dark beauty of it, where there were questions to find answers to, or not, where there were patterns and randomness, where life and death relied on each other to grow, to thrive, to be.

Angling

She woke one morning—after a dream about her fisherman friend, Van, who'd died too young—with the sensation of a hook snagged on the inside of her cheek, close to her lip. Like a piece of fishing line attached from her drooped mouth to him, wherever he lingered now.

Her son didn't catch it at first, and when she slurred, "Does my mouth look right," he answered, "Yeah, you look fine, Mom." But he also wrinkled his brows and turned his eyes to his father, saying, in a tone she rarely heard now that he was growing into a man, "Daaaad."

Her husband worried she'd stroked. Her father had one, and her grandfather, grandmother, and three uncles. He called 911, promised he'd be right behind her, and before they lifted her into the ambulance, he kissed her good side.

The doctor assured, "It's not a stroke. It's temporary."

"What about my eye?" she asked. "It won't stop crying."

He marked, with a lopsided star, "excessive tearing" on the list of symptoms he handed her. "Two weeks. You'll be back to normal."

But she knew what happened. Van had caught her again, just when she thought she'd been healed of him, and she peered out the window as her husband drove them back home along that winding flooded creek bed of the Sidle where she'd once talked too much and spooked the rainbow and brook trout, sending them into deeper runs.

Had Van used a dressed treble hook, meant to lure her with its flashy feathers, or a siwash, meant to leave her less damaged by his memory, or a jig hook to ensure the set?

She could see his smile, his eyes, almost touch his fingers again as he crimped five split shot to the line to weight it down.

After the two weeks her doctor promised, her face righted and Van's face faded again, rippled back to blurs, caught deep in a backcast, tangled in a tree she couldn't find.

You Four Are the One

What Cinta Johns needed was someone to make her tea after her husband left for work so she didn't have to get up from the recliner. Steep it for exactly three minutes, add one tablespoon of clover honey. No more. Just one tablespoon. Miss Jean promised it would help with her congestion. What Cinta Johns needed was to have someone rub the fading, chipping, blood-red paint from her toenails, paint them a color that would not remind her of all the things that could go wrong.

What Cinta Johns needed was someone to walk her dog, Sheppy, four times a day, or more if possible. Sheppy, at thirteen, had an active bladder like Cinta, in her condition at thirty-three. No way could she get down on her knees and scrub the floor if Sheppy had accidents. And she wouldn't ask anyone else—"No, no!"—she couldn't ask anyone to clean up her dog's pee! What she needed was someone to take the wet clothes out to the line—she loved the scent of summer, tree bark, grass cuttings on her shirts and sheets. And if it threatened to rain to please, please, quickly take them down, fold them if they were properly dry, put them all away. Neatly. More than ever before, she needed everything to be organized and categorized and ordered.

What Cinta Johns needed was for people to come into her home or sit with her under the big oak and entertain her if she was sad, take her mind off the baby for bits of time.

Which was strange.

Because it's all we could possibly think about, that baby. How long it would live inside Cinta Johns, how big it was getting, how much its lungs had grown. Everyone all kinds of worried about those lungs.

What Cinta Johns needed, our moms said, was much less pressure to deliver this baby healthy and ready for this world. Losing four babies in seven years. Too much pressure for this one. We were sent to help in any way we could.

But we—Tessa, Dawn, Billie, and me, Lanie—were only four neighbor girls who'd just watched the "Menstruation Movie" but didn't know all the possible snags and hitches of pregnancy. It was the summer before our sixth-grade year and we had to steady ourselves to not be dizzy, to not be nervous, to pace ourselves with all these new words we'd heard from the eavesdropped conversations of our teachers who were Cinta Johns's old friends, from the mouths of our moms and the neighborhood women who'd been closely monitoring her pregnancy. They'd said things like "She's sure to lose this one, too," and "What a pity" and "It's just not in the cards for her to be a mother" and "Made it almost full term with that last little one, but then . . ." They talked of a dilated cervix, contractions and preterm labor, steroid shots, some drug called Brethine, and all these awful ideas about undeveloped lungs and brains.

What Cinta Johns needed was someone to hold her hand. She told us that when we showed up at her house, her eyes wet and red. "Just hold my hand for a minute." And we could do that. Yes, for sure, we could do that.

That first week of her Strict Bedrest, we stood at the base of her old black oak, the lichen-dressed side. Hemmed in around Cinta Johns. Captured by her smallish hill of a pregnant belly, we waited, quiet as cobwebs, as she stilled herself within the cradled macramé hammock. Her manicured hands—matte pink nail beds, arctic white tips—rested over our filthy ones, nails jam-packed with the blackest soil from filching night crawlers to ensure a trout harvest for Cinta Johns and her growing baby inside her.

She guided our palms across her belly, said, "Wait, wait, wait. The baby's readying to kick."

The neighbors had started hand-thinning their fruit trees, and Nonna, my great-grandma, far too old to climb a ladder, troubled by the lace bugs on her azaleas, planned to include our "buoni occhi," our good eyes, in her insect war. She yelled over the hedge from our house, white hair lifting in the wind, "You bring me ladybugs. Many, many!"

She'd have to wait. No time for gathering lace bug-eating ladybugs.

And then it happened. Like the ground swell some long-snouted mole might push up through perfectly hard dirt, that baby's foot or knee or elbow heaved up. Our heads buzzed. Spots swirled our eyes as we held our hands against Cinta Johns's bare warm belly skin. We might have passed out, had Cinta not clutched us with her smile. "Feel that?"

Yes, we did.

Feeling that baby moving filled us with so much hope. We knew we weren't ever going to let this baby die. Too many deaths had already come to our neighborhood, in person and in place. Old Mr. Riggle, who was the same exact age as Nonna, had a heart attack while planting his onion sets in the spring. Rollo's chocolate shop had caught fire, likely wouldn't ever be built back up, and the Polish deli that had been selling the best pierogi and halušky since Nonna was my age had gone out of business. The Baker twins' two beagle dogs got some virus that killed them.

That baby's kick gave us all the spirit we needed to repaint Cinta Johns's white yard fence, the whole way around the back, while Sheppy rolled in the grass and sniffed squirrel and rabbit poop, even ate some. It gave us the strength to move at least a hundred ton of gravel from around the shrubs and hostas Cinta's husband was transplanting to make room for a family swing with a canopy, a future play area for the baby. It gave us the steady hands to paint, in the tiniest detail, each of the bird boxes with Cinta Johns's favorite flowers—dwarf irises and lily-of-the-valley.

All of this was much more exciting than being at the pool and trying to ignore everyone bikinied who'd "developed," all that comparing that would surely happen. At Cinta Johns's house we weren't four flat-chested nerdy girls in one pieces. We were a part of her Support Team that, according to Mom, included Cinta's husband— when he wasn't at the mill—our moms and aunts, and even Nonna, though she was totally preoccupied with her garlic falling over, worrying which curses would hit her gardens sent by the woman across the river and her "il malocchio," her evil eye.

⌇

"The baby's hiccupping," Cinta said as she fiddled with the lighter. Then she touched the fire to our sparklers, ones we'd saved over from the Fourth of July special for this day. It was the twenty-eighth week—the beginning of the Third Trimester, a big deal to Cinta's doctor. But I was still thinking about those dang undeveloped lungs as everyone else was oohing and aahing because, according to my mom, the baby would likely still have to go to the NICU if it was born this early.

"It's about the size of a head of cauliflower!" Cinta cheered. Everyone but me whooped. A head of cauliflower could be many sizes, really small, as I'd seen with Nonna's when she'd placed plants too close together. When compared to a small watermelon, which is where everyone wanted that baby to be, a cauliflower head, even a regular-sized one, was a ways off.

When I got home that night, I asked Mom how big she thought the baby might be. She said it wasn't as much the size as it was the organs inside being healthy.

"Don't worry. The baby's come far," Nonna said, immediately blessing herself, which always made me nervous. But it was true. The baby had developed a lot since that last day of school when the four of us overheard the school nurse explaining to our teacher at recess that Cinta Johns was in preterm labor, that she had to have pills to keep the contractions from continuing, to keep her uterus from pushing her baby out too early. "Only twenty-three weeks. Poor

Cinta." "Baby would have to be rushed to the NICU in the city. Would have a low rate of survival. Again." "What a shame. She's gonna need help with cleaning, and that dog!" "Has to stay flat for the rest of the pregnancy. Not even allowed up and down stairs." "Yes, how will she keep up her house? Make meals?"

"Babies come when they ready, see, when they ready," Nonna said after Mom tried to explain how the steroid shots would help grow the baby's lungs. Nonna wasn't a fan of those shots and all the medicines Cinta had to take.

"Well," Mom said, staring out the window at Cinta's husband as he unloaded lumber from his truck, "thank goodness he's working late. He'd better get that nursery ready in case that baby's ready to come."

"Oh, he's a love. He's a peach," Nonna said, pushing Mom aside so she could better see him. She loved Cinta Johns's husband. "He's so good to me. He brings me those especial olives from The Strip District. Remember?"

"That nursery's not even started by the looks of it," my mom said. "That baby could come any time now." She stopped scrubbing the pans. Shook her head.

The baby wasn't due until late September, on my birthday. I'd been envied a little because of that fact, and it was about time. Tessa, Dawn, and Billie all shared February birthdays, all Aquarians, a point they loved to make that bittered my stomach nearly as much as Nonna's dandelion salads. I was the lone Virgo. Not only that, they all had names that began with letters that rhymed. We were the TDBL club. T for Tessa, D for Dawn, B for Billie, and L for me, Lanie. Even Cinta rhymed them with C. The CTDBL club. I was the oddball. As usual.

September 22 was still far away. Cinta's husband had time to finish the room, I dared to say, but I swallowed the words.

"He's not punched out through the back wall yet for the add-on," my mom barked, like it was her walls he needed to sledge through. "And he's adding on a bathroom, too. All that plumbing that will need to be rerouted, the sewage."

~

When we girls showed up at Cinta's the next day, I warned everyone that this construction needed to happen ASAP. There we stood, watching her husband, willing him to please GET TO IT ALREADY. We even told him we'd help, and he patted our heads like we were five years old and said, "I got this."

He shoveled down his supper, kissed Cinta full on the mouth, for God's sake, and stared at her eyes for well over ten seconds. He laid his hands on her belly, then he laid his cheek on it, then, finally, thank the Lord, he went upstairs to change his clothes, came back downstairs and put on his ragged old sneakers, and headed to the back of the house.

I was so relieved to hear the saw whining through the wood, the hammer pounding. We scraped off his plate into Sheppy's bowl, banged the dirt off his work boots, and found the pork roast in the deep freeze to thaw in the fridge for a Crock-Pot meal the next day. We'd planned to sleep out at Cinta Johns's that night—maybe the whole weekend. It was going to be a full moon. We set up our tent in her backyard.

It was still so sickening hot by the nine o'clock curfew whistle and Cinta's husband was still at it. Pounding and sawing.

"When do you suppose he'll have it done?" I asked Cinta as I opened up the containers of cut carrots and dip we'd prepared for our evening snack. We were officially eating only colorful fruits and vegetables in front of her. The baby, in addition to wanting out early, had somehow given her sugar-diabetes. Who knew how that could happen to a perfectly healthy person? So she had to prick her finger two hours after each meal and first thing in the morning. She had to eat small meals every three and a half hours. Thank goodness it was summer vacation. I'd already begun worrying about how she'd get herself snacks every three hours when we were back at school and her husband at work. My mom said Nonna could take care of that, not to worry, but Nonna was so preoccupied with the curses on her garden and come end of August, when the peaches and tomatoes were ready, she'd be obsessed with canning. She'd be a complete and total mess.

Cinta didn't seem worried one bit about the project. "He said if he has no setbacks with the plumbing, he could have it done and the walls ready to paint by the end of August," she said. "If he doesn't have to stay for overtime at work."

"That should work, I guess," I said and quickly volunteered us for the painting job. I could have been wrong but Tessa and Dawn looked for a brief moment as if they weren't excited about the painting. But Billie nodded, said she had her own roller from painting her bedroom in the spring.

The whole way through July, Cinta had been getting restless, no wonder. She wanted to stay outside later and later each evening. We were allowed to stick around as long as she wanted us and she kept saying, "Stay" and "What's your hurry?" She loved our stories.

She seemed to be scared to be alone with her own mind. I completely understood that.

So we lounged with her outside watching those busy lightning bugs. And while I could not pinch the glowing guts out and make rings for her, the other three did, and even spread the glowing guts on her belly, lighting up stars over the hill that held the baby. Oh, did that baby kick when they did that, but I worried that it wasn't proper at all to be hurting bugs, even killing them, given we were trying here to save a whole life!

The next day I saw I was right. Killing all those fireflies angered the mosquitoes. Our legs were covered with raised red bites. They hit Cinta far worse than us and all told she had hundreds just on her legs alone.

"Imagine having to lay still all day long and then have all those mosquito bites on top of that?" my mom said to Nonna.

"Zucchero," Nonna said, nodding her head, raising her white brows.

"The diabetes doesn't make mosquitoes bite more," Mom said. And then to me, "It's not true. Don't worry."

But Mom didn't seem convinced by her own words, and I suddenly felt thirsty. Maybe I had sugar, too?

The next day, Nonna was panicked. "Call Cinta now, see if she's alla-right!" Nonna had heard a screech owl in the night, thought she might be dreaming, but heard it square in the morning, too. She had issues with birds. She was convinced Old Mr. Riggle died, because the day before, a cardinal had crashed into his kitchen window, broke its little neck. She wept when she heard the pair of rock doves, said their cooing to each other made her miss grandad. "He wanta me with him in Heaven." But the way she flipped over that owl, yelling, "Oh, that tremolo. It sings out, a death to come soon. Il gufo, il gufo!" and rummaged through the cupboard to find her iron skillet, shook us all up. "Tocca, tocca!" she cried, made us touch the iron for good luck.

Outside, the backup alarm called us to the window. An ambulance. At Cinta Johns's house. "Oh no. That poor baby." Nonna held up her hands. Mom pushed a chair behind her, made her sit down.

~

We had to wait all day to hear what had happened.

"She'll be fine. She's real strong," Cinta's husband said, flashed a solid smile. Not one bit fake. "The new medicine they're giving her at the hospital lowers calcium in her uterus's cells, I guess. To stop contractions. Mag-ne-si-um sul-fate."

"Oh," I said. The four of us clomped down the rickety wood steps behind him.

"But it heats her up. Like a fever or something. One of the side effects."

Something? Is it a fever or not? We stood in their basement. Smelled like some cross between fresh-cut pine boards, mice droppings, dirt, and pennies. Spiderwebs everywhere. A drip-drop sound coming from somewhere.

He screwed the blowtorch onto the propane canister. His hands shook like Cinta's did on that first medicine, the Brethine. I noticed he was sweating like crazy, too. He was not the certain kind of handsome like on TV shows, in magazine ads. It was his kindness that drew me to watch his face as he told us about Cinta's condition. It's what had drawn me, too, to his broad shoulders and muscular arms—especially when he'd lifted Cinta and carried her through the house, up the stairs, two nights before, while we ran ahead, turned down the bed for her. She laughed, said, "I'm not an invalid," but he'd said, "Doc wants you recumbent and we are working hard to keep you that way." He'd winked at us then, told us how much he appreciated our help. And I'd noticed his arms, too, when he'd lifted Sheppy onto the couch when Sheppy couldn't make his legs spring right. Triceps. Like some unripe hard pear was settled under the skin of his upper arms. I did not have that muscle. But I started doing pushups when I saw his in order to grow muscles like that.

"They're keeping her all weekend." He looked up at the greened and pitted pipes above us. "They have to keep a close eye on her, so the hospital's the best place to be."

I stood beside him, staring at lengths of copper pipe and tons of little elbows.

"Why'd she go into labor again? Did they say?" I asked.

"They don't really know." He picked up a copper fitting. "So, I need all these wire-brushed. Once I cut the pipe in the lengths I need, you'll take this emery paper, see, rub the ends 'til they look like this, okay?"

But how could he just leave her at the hospital? We could've watched Sheppy. Shouldn't he be there?

"No. It's best she rests much as she can. I'm better off here getting this nursery ready."

We scratched at our mosquito bites, wire-brushed the fittings while he worked. "You watch you don't get cut on those ends," he warned.

How could I concentrate on anything but Cinta and all her mosquito bites, Cinta and her poor baby? Plumbing was the boring-est job.

Until.

That scrape, scrape of the igniter to the blowtorch. The blue flame flaring out, turned down to a pointy burn. Downright magical watching him heat up those joints, then, at just the right time, that stick of silver solder became bead and pulled right up into those joints, liquefied into a perfect ring around the copper. Silent, we stood there. Soon watching that flame reminded me that Cinta would be heating up, too, with a fever. At the hospital. Maybe scared to be all alone, hooked up to an IV—the worst fate ever, an IV in your hand. Would they have a bucket for her to be sick in? What if she passed out walking to the restroom in the dark of the night? What if she pulled her IV out?

We discussed all of this and more on our walk home along the alley lit up by the full moon we'd hoped to watch with Cinta. We'd planned to stay over again in the tent. But something about Cinta hooked up in a bed not her own made me ache for mine. I said, "Hey, let's plan another night." They tried to talk me into it, but I insisted I wanted to go home.

A white shadowed thing was crossing the alley. Skunk? No. Maybe Shafer's cat hunting? No. It was a possum. It stopped as we closed in. Had a little one on its back. Still hanging on in July. Nonna would surely say it was an "il presagio," an omen of something worrisome to come.

While everyone else was squealing, "Ah, how cute," I was sure it was a bad sign. Cinta was going to lose her baby.

"No, she won't," Billie said.

"No. Don't cry," Tessa said. "You know how much we're helping her. She's going to be fine."

I collapsed right down in the alley.

"Hey. It's okay," Dawn said. "You're gonna throw up crying that hard. You have to stop. It's okay. Try to think about something happy."

But I couldn't. All I could think about was if Cinta had never stayed outside with us she'd never have gotten mosquito bites, which I now knew were definitely the cause of her going back into labor. That or the gutted fireflies.

"Cinta's husband said straight out that it had nothing to do with that," Dawn said. Tessa bobbed her head in agreement. Billie didn't seem so sure.

But what if it did?

I scratched my bites then. They all said, "NO, DON'T! You'll scar!"

But I didn't care if I bloodied and scarred my whole body. If we'd somehow done something to cause this, well, we should all be in pain.

And it felt so good to scratch.

~

Well.

Mr. Carli saw the ghost of his old boss at the coal tipple, ten years after he died. "Mr. Carli guilt-shocked himself," my mom said. Nonna said, "Carli did that man wrong." And she believed the ghost of his boss was there to remind him to be honest.

And the Baker twins who never married and lived in their old homestead at the edge of the river hill said their dead beagles came back in the night sometimes, aching to hunt a rabbit. "See," they showed us, "lookie at that hole they dug, wanting a nest." But they pulled the bills of their hats low to keep their eyebrows from showing their lies. Nonna said she'd heard those dogs barking. "Left in pens, too much," she said. "They come back, sure. But not for rabbits. They come bite those twins one these nights on they shins in they sleep."

Mrs. Bianco saw her husband in the attic. Dead thirty-six years. Sorting through photos. Still forty years old, same age as when he had the heart attack. "Well, no, he didn't say a word, just pointed to a photo. Then vanished." She showed us the photo she'd hung next to their wedding portrait. Nothing special, really. An orange pickup her husband drove to deliver eggs. He wasn't even in the photo. I looked closer to see if there was some message there. Nothing.

And Mr. Wiles, our old fourth-grade teacher, said his father came to him five years after he died while Mr. Wiles was fishing at Sidle Creek. Said he had only two words. "Live full." Mr. Wiles quit his job in the machine shop, ears turning to mush from the sounds of it, and became a teacher. His bulletin boards were jammed full of quotes about living life right, to the fullest, without regret, intentionally. Why would he lie about those words?

Nonna believed everyone's sightings because she was connected. "Sono connesso agli spirito." And because her dead mother traveled with her everywhere. Sat in the garden beside her, choosing which zucchini flowers to batter and fry. She stood at the stove and made sure Nonna spiced them right. Nonna would talk to her, nod to her, laugh with her. Which seemed crazy. But nice, too.

We wished it would happen to us, a ghost sighting, but none of us had seen more than a shadow in our bedrooms at night that turned out to be, when the lights flicked on, nothing more than the streetlight's trick or a robe on a hook, the funny shapes on a poster.

So we believed Cinta Johns when she said her mother came back to her. Stood right beside her hospital bed.

"I couldn't get my breath. I couldn't reach the button for the nurse. I couldn't sit up. My arms and legs almost rock, so heavy."

"What did you do?"

"I guess I called for my mother. Because there she was. To my left. She was wearing her aqua blue blouse, sleeves rolled up to three quarter, and her gold bracelet with the anchor on it, and a white pencil skirt and heels. She had her hair parted on the side like always and her favorite pearl earrings. She looked wonderful, you know? Not one bit sick from the chemo. And she told me she'd help me."

I could almost see her mom, even though I'd never met her, but I had to know, "Did she say those words? I'll help you."

"Yes, and she said she'd keep sending me people, helpers," Cinta said. "And the nurse came. Gave me more oxygen." Cinta sipped her water, then said, "She sent you girls here to help me." She rubbed her hand over her belly. "And now my baby is doing great." She started crying then. "I'm okay. Just emotional is all. I'm okay."

But watching the tears pour out of her like that made me wonder just how okay she really was. I often said I was okay when I cried like that. And I really wasn't okay at all.

I woke Nonna through the night and asked if what Cinta said could be true, that her dead mom sent *us* to help Cinta.

She sat straight up, not one bit sleepy, and said, "Oh yes. Sua madre, her mama, she came, she woke up in you girls that nurture." She pushed her knuckles into my sternum.

I didn't pull away. It was true. There was something right there, a nurture in the middle of my chest, wanting to help Cinta Johns.

⌣

It took three full weeks after Cinta returned from that magnesium sulfate weekend for the itchiness from those bites to stop. She'd scratched some of hers so bad I worried she'd surely get an infection. Sometimes she'd cry while we put calamine lotion on all of those dots and say things like, "You girls are stars. You girls are the best thing in my life." She became full-out sad, crying at anything.

"Just the hormones," Mom kept saying.

Even her flower gardens got her crying. "Look at them," she'd say, and I didn't know if she was happy or sad about the fact that every single flower in her garden was blooming. I wasn't allowed to pick perennials any other time, but this summer my mom said, "Cut some and prepare them in vases for her end tables and bed stand, her kitchen table. It will brighten her day." So we cut hydrangeas and daylilies and daisies. It worked. "Thank you so much. You all could be interior decorators someday!"

When I asked her if her mom had come back again, she shook her head, looked like she might cry. So I didn't dare ask a second time. But I wondered, especially when I'd see her staring up into the oak. It seemed a perfect place for her mom to sit, right up there within the rock dove nest, along those sturdy thick branches.

⌣

Dew started up its nighttime spread, glazing the grass, wetting our heads. Low night bugs became a hum of old rosary women before Mass. The peppermint oil Nonna had given us to keep the mosquitoes away burned our eyes, made them water awful. The blurry altered shadows in the yard. Frightening what-ifs took up in our heads. And that sound of something moving?

Half laughing at our hyper minds, we all jumped when our flashlight beams caught the eyes.

The mother possum. It had been almost a whole month since we'd seen her on the alley. She strolled through, halted at the firepit, hunkered down. Her baby possum hung on for dear life.

Both sets of eyes glowed in our beams.

"Don't blind them! Don't scare them!" I whispered, and the darn thing cocked its head.

Closer it came.

A few steps. But enough to alert us that it was either a magical possum or it was rabid. No night animal ever walks toward you, unless it's a coyote. We all screamed at once, ran to my house.

"Yes, poor thing. It may be rabid? I'm not really sure. I'll tell your father," my mom said, peering out the kitchen window.

"No," Nonna said. "He not shoot it!"

She rushed us to the living room. She grabbed my shoulders tight, said, "A sign. That possum."

"I know it was a sign, but a sign of what?" I asked.

A jumble of Italian and English words spilled into the room as she waved her hands in the air, clapped, held her fists up. More what-ifs. What if the placentas from Cinta's four dead babies—Nonna herself had instructed Cinta's husband to bury them under their fruit trees—had become guardian angels? What if those angels were working through the four of us? "Uno, due, tre, quattro." She tapped each of us on the head with her knuckle. We rubbed our heads.

Nonna clapped again, clearly thrilled about this possum, and she moved to the rolltop desk, pulled out her notebook I was never allowed to read, her favorite pen. We were forced to sit on the couch while she slowly named and wrote: "Fresha gingaroot, redda rassaberry leafs, fresha crannaberry, mint, rosa hips, honey, thyme, basilico, and most, MOST, garlic! I make a necklace, just in case!"

She said we must round it all up early the next morning to make "new and especial teas and snacks" for Cinta Johns. We must not be lazy and sleep in. Early morning we must get up. "Help chop!" She said, "We know now. For sure. You have been called. You four are the one."

Billie elbowed me. I repeated the word *called* in my head over and over. A small gasp wanted to burst out my mouth but I held it back. Dawn squeezed my hand. Tessa said, "But—"

"Nonna. For pity's sake, stop." Mom stomped into the living room. "Look! You're scaring them." But Nonna sat her down between us on the couch. She rattled fast Italian for three whole minutes without taking a breath.

Mom stood, clasped her hands with Nonna's, said, "You're right. There's a lot we can still do. What can it hurt?"

Nonna nodded hard. Once. She clapped her hands, said, "Buona notte!"

Once Nonna was halfway up the stairs, Mom told us what we'd been doing all summer was helping Cinta Johns a lot. She said the mosquitoes, the possum, all this was simply a coincidence. "You need only do what's fun for you, okay?" she said, and wrinkled her brow to our silence. "Hey, how 'bout I take you all to Monty's pool tomorrow? Or Buttermilk Falls?" She said she'd drive us to Bell's to get the best ice cream.

But I said, "No, we want to make teas." Dawn seemed disappointed, but when I scowled at her, she nodded in agreement.

"Okay," Mom said. "Okay." And she kissed each of our heads and told us we could stay up late and watch movies. She'd make popcorn. "Don't worry, okay?" she said.

~

We made Cinta's tea sachets and delivered them to her pantry, along with Nonna's instruction sheet.

"Nonna is brilliant," Cinta said.

The next day Nonna insisted we help her with her seeds from her first round of tomatoes. She'd already pulped them and let them ferment—the smell made me half sick when I walked through the garage. It was certainly no wonder stray cats steered clear of our place. I had to sniff my shirts every time I left the house just to make sure I didn't smell like fermenting tomato seeds. She wanted them ready. She was always getting something ready for some time in the future, planning her planting, mulching, everything had to do with the next season. One year she hadn't planted new tulip bulbs and chipmunks ate up the old ones. Still there were tulips come spring but there might not have been. She was all about planning. Being prepared.

I stood at the sink and watched the moldy pulp wash away, watched the mature seeds stick in the bottom of the strainer. We laid them out on paper plates to dry. It would take a whole month for them to dry completely. It seemed like such a stupid thing to do. All this waiting was horrible. Nonna said, "Always think ahead, good, but you must be patient, too. La Pazienza È la Virtù dei Forti!"

Cinta Johns, too, was getting frustrated with the waiting. She said she wished she could do cartwheels with us. Roundoffs. So we did competitions for her. She judged us on our form.

The activity that always seemed to help Cinta with her nerves, with her frustrations, with her stress, was listening to music. She loved, especially, old songs, so we set up her ancient tape deck on the small table beside her pitcher of iced water, strung an electric cord from the house, made sure Sheppy didn't trip on it, and we listened to songs Cinta knew every word to. Luckily, the choruses were all catchy and we hummed along. Linda Ronstadt's "Poor Poor Pitiful Me" and the Eagles whole *Hotel California* album—Cinta particularly loved "The Last Resort." It made her tear up a little. We all yelled out the lyrics to ABBA's "Dancing Queen," which Billie and I did actually know quite well, while Cinta snapped her fingers above her belly. We acted like we were waltzing with Sheppy.

Cinta's husband was fixing the leaking downspout when the song "Handy Man" came on. Cinta almost tipped herself out of the hammock trying to turn it up. Her husband climbed down the ladder, singing right along with her. I wasn't a James Taylor fan. He was one of many male songwriters that my mom loved, but whose songs I thought were too depressing. But when I heard the words as Cinta and her husband sang them, as I watched him lean down and kiss Cinta, a long one but not so gross, I might have started to change my mind. Suddenly James Taylor's voice encircled the tree, spread through the yard. Everyone was giggling, and I could tell Cinta wanted to break the biggest rule of all, get out of that hammock and slow dance with her husband who was now swaying, holding Cinta's hand.

He wanted that, too. I could tell.

I wouldn't have it—the pain of watching them want to dance, but needing that baby safe, too. I thought I might choke, my throat was hurting so. I thought I might cry.

What could be done?

Cinta nodded toward me and her husband turned, came closer, held out his hand. I jumped up before I even really knew what the heck I was doing and suddenly I was twirling under his arm. He let go, held out his hand to Tessa. Tessa, whose mom and dad had gotten divorced at Christmas, who hadn't really laughed in any more than a fake giggle since, was suddenly uncontrolled glee. Then to Dawn. Shyest Dawn, who broke out in hives if a boy came near her, allowed her forced ballerina classes her rich aunt insisted she take to work their magic. She was all stage and beauty, her arms perfectly glamourous, flowing. Then to Billie, who'd almost failed the school year from too many sick days, suffered terrible with a nervous belly, lost her pale sickly color, and when Cinta's husband dipped Billie, Tessa and Dawn and Cinta cheered.

I was stunned by the whole scene.

He came back to me again and I twirled once more, feeling summer air on my face, looking up through the oak tree's canopy into the sun. I could hear lawnmowers over the music, and everyone's laughter. Sheppy barking.

Cinta's husband let go of my hand and in one elegant move, he lifted Cinta from the hammock, danced them in circles. Sheppy got the zoomies and ran and jumped, barking louder.

Cinta's husband was more handsome than a man should ever be allowed. I wanted to be twirled a third time, a fourth. Instead, we four girls lopped our arms over each other's shoulders and swayed as a rope chain. I was assured, right then, that even though he was busy all the time with hammering and sawing, soldering and drilling, patching and painting, Cinta's husband's favorite job was simply being Cinta's husband.

I didn't want him to settle her back into the hammock. I didn't want that song to ever end.

It was like I was flying into the sky, a swallow, and I looked down through the oak and saw Nonna staring into her azalea leaves, Mom walking out to the mailbox, stopping to talk with Mrs. Bianco about the fundraiser for the church, the Baker twins plucking burrs off their dogs from the morning rabbit run in the thick brush at the beagle club like they'd miraculously come back to life. I could see the Sidle Creek and Mr. Wiles fishing there. I could see our winding Allegheny River and the pontoons filled with people partying together. I could see us in Cinta's yard, her husband spinning her around, all four of us, a lacing of girls swaying, poor Sheppy zooming with his butt tucked down, throughout the yard.

~

That night I couldn't fall asleep. Mom came in to turn off my music, said, "Hey, what's this?" I'd piled about three thousand of my used tissues on my nightstand. I couldn't stop crying if I'd wanted to. "What's wrong?"

I tried to tell her how beautiful Cinta and her husband were together, how much her husband clearly loved her, how much I wanted this baby to live, how it wasn't fair that their other ones didn't, and what if this one died, too?

And my mom said, "Then they'll go on. These things happen."

"But why?"

"Well, that's not for us to say. But listen. From the sound of it and from what I've seen, I think they'll be okay. After all, they have each other, right?"

"Right."

But it wouldn't be right at all. Mom's shirt smelled like popcorn and fabric softener and her arms pulled me tighter than they had in a while. And I don't know why but I had to ask, "Why don't you and dad ever dance together?" I was angry and sad and not sure what else I was feeling. I guess I just wanted to know everyone and everything was going to be all right.

She said, "Well, we certainly know how." And she might have gone to bed and left me there to think things through, left me with her regular, "It will all seem better in the morning." She said, "Get up, Lanie, come on."

I followed her to the living room where Nonna, weirdly still awake, sat there tatting. Dad was drinking a beer and watching the eleven o'clock news. Mom whispered something to him and then something to Nonna, and Nonna waved her away and laughed. But then Mom turned the TV down and put on one of her favorite songs. Patsy Cline's "You Belong to Me." Which wasn't nearly as cool as James Taylor's "Handy Man" but Dad stood up right away, and he held her just so, and they moved around the living room like they were gliding on an ice skating rink. I'd never seen them like this. Normally, they were in each other's way both in words and deeds.

I started up my crying all over again.

Nonna set down her needle and thread and stood, held out her hands to me. "Alzarsi! Danza, danza!" Nonna spun me under her arm like Cinta's husband had. And while it wasn't beneath the oak in the sunshine and the song wasn't the same, I still felt like the world was a good place to be and that I wasn't alone. I thought of Tessa at her mom's, her dad at his new girlfriend's place up north, he forgetting sometimes to call Tessa back. I thought of Dawn who'd said when she couldn't sleep, she wasn't allowed to "wake the house" so she'd go to the basement and curl up on her dog's bed until morning. I thought of Billie who said she had to shut the lights on and off seventeen times before she could climb into bed and rest. And I thought of Cinta and how she'd said that more babies are born during the night than in the day and she was afraid she wouldn't wake up when her water finally broke.

I tried to stay right there, dancing with Nonna, trying not to think about a time when Nonna wouldn't be here, trying not to think about that baby dying, trying not to let my mind race all over the place.

~

A week before the first day of our sixth-grade year, every part of Cinta Johns's house, yard, buzzed. Our moms painted the nursery and the new bathroom, hung shelves, set up the crib and changing table, and organized—according to Cinta's needs—all the supplies for the new baby that people had gifted her at the shower. I'd spent that whole baby shower, the day before, making sure Cinta drank enough water. She'd looked so pretty in her sunshine yellow dress lined with faint tiny pineapple designs, lounging on the maroon velvet, the fainting couch Mrs. Bianco had the Baker twins carry over from her parlor and settle under the big oak. Cinta Johns had hit thirty-five weeks but she still had to be "as recumbent as possible." Recumbent, as a word, sounded horrible, and so did Strict Bedrest, but it had worked all summer. She'd followed the doctor's rules. Took no chances. "About five more weeks to go," she said, untying the ribbons from Sheppy's neck that had donned all the beautiful packages of tiny clothes, tiny blankets, booties, hats, she'd opened the day before.

Everyone sweated relief that the baby had made it so far. Gardeners in the neighborhood, including Nonna, were sure their bounty was keeping Cinta and the baby healthy. The women of the neighborhood had made sure Cinta would be ready once the baby got here, and it did seem, in doing this, they were convinced that this time, a healthy birth was bound to happen.

I knew we four girls were doing everything we could think of to keep Cinta happy, to keep her from being stressed out with worry over the baby. We'd been helping her laugh, and according to her doctor, laughter really did help, was really some sort of best medicine. Also, being close to a person, hugging them, holding their hand, talking, apparently raised up certain hormones called Ox-y-to-cin that helped the body in unimaginable ways. Weird as it sounded, there was science to prove it. And yet, I didn't feel the relief that everyone else was feeling at all. I guessed I wouldn't until that baby was born right.

Mom kept saying she thought it might be best to concentrate on school. She'd wave new markers and pencils and notebooks in front of me, but even the scent of new erasers didn't do me any good.

Mom kept saying it might be best to get some new outfits, even though I strangely hadn't grown out of anything, like every year before. No floods jeans. All cuffs still met my wrists. My toes weren't squished into the ends of my sneakers. "We can go tomorrow!"

"That's okay," I said. "I don't need anything."

Mom kept saying it might be fun to tie-dye shirts with leftovers from Nonna's garden.

So two days before school began, we gathered at Cinta's kitchen, ladled over our banded shirts and Cinta's banded onesie the turmeric dye and beet dye mom had made ahead of time with

Nonna. It was kind of boring, to be honest, little kid's stuff, but the next day, when we opened up our ziplock bags, cut the bands off, unrolled and flattened out our designs, I was shocked. "They are magnificent!" I said. Mom and Nonna clapped and oohed, but Cinta started to cry when Mom held up the onesie.

"It's okay," Mom said, but Cinta shook her head like it wasn't, like there was something huge she needed to get out of her.

Nonna held her hand over Cinta's heart, recited some words in Italian I didn't understand. Then she said, "This baby be just fine. You know it. God make this baby stick 'round, grow perfect inside you. You see." She pointed up, said, "He listen to me." Then she spit on the floor and stomped. We all stood there petrified, waiting for something in the kitchen to blow up or for the oak tree to uproot and fall on the house because Nonna had actually said God listened to her. But nothing happened and Cinta wiped her tears away and kissed Nonna's cheek. "Thank you. Thank you all so much."

"Why don't you girls go lay these out on the picnic table so they dry completely," Mom said. But I didn't want to leave Cinta when she needed us the most.

Outside, I lingered near the window, heard Cinta's voice, so small, saying, "I'm scared. I've come this far and—"

"You will deal with whatever comes. We'll be here to help you, okay," Mom murmured and stroked Cinta's long, wavy brown hair, and I couldn't have been more relieved she was my mom, relieved she hadn't died young like Cinta's mom. I knew she meant it. If she said she'd be there for you, she was.

"Thank Lanie and the girls for me. I can't tell you how much they've helped me this summer."

"I will, love. Now don't you worry. We are almost there, okay?"

That my mom said "we" instead of "you" made me smile. Sheppy must have heard, too, because he was smiling his German shepherd crooked teeth at me as I stood under the window eavesdropping.

~

I tried my best to be excited for the first day of school. But while we had a plan to wear our tie-dye shirts, Tessa's mom insisted she wear the new jumper she'd made for her, Dawn's mom wanted her to match her brothers in the outfits her rich aunt sent them, Billie's mom said she looked peaked in those tie-dye colors and forced her to wear the ugliest cream-colored frilly blouse—of all things? In the end, once we all got to our sixth-grade room, we matched. I felt so blessed that they'd smashed their shirts into their backpacks and changed in the restroom before the announcements began.

We had to hear about all the great awards and accomplishments everyone but us had all summer. The swim and diving teams, the gymnastics squad, the boys' Little League. No one announced that we'd spent all summer doing errands and keeping calm a woman in a Complicated and High-Risk Pregnancy, that we'd been saving a baby from being born too early. I thought that was a horrible oversight and I told our new sixth-grade teacher at recess. It was a risk. She was new, had never met the four of us, but she'd heard about us from our fifth-grade teacher. "All good things," she said. Then, she added, "I'll see what I can do for tomorrow. What is the woman's name?"

"Cinta Johns. And she's due on September 22. My birthday."

"Okay. I'll see if we can make some kind of announcement."

While I wasn't thrilled about being back, I had my suspicions that this woman might be the best kind of teacher. One with a sense of justice, who made time to hear your words, who treated you like you were some kind of important in the world.

"Maybe we can make that announcement when the baby is born," she added. But the way she said "when," with emphasis, sounded a little off, like she didn't believe it would happen.

Those first two weeks, though, much as I tried, I couldn't concentrate. The neighbor ladies were doing a great job taking care of Cinta Johns and Nonna sat with her in the evenings while we did our homework. And while Cinta wasn't judging our competitions or singing songs or laughing at our stories, she seemed awfully content with Nonna, who'd started teaching her to tat. Which, despite everything I thought of it up to that point, was beginning to look sort of interesting.

Nonna forced us to help her with her fall planting. Radishes and more leafy lettuce, kohlrabi. "Dig, dig! Don't a be lazy!"

The fall boat show bleated from the river a few miles away. The ice cream Jeep guy drove his final run, trying to get us to buy up his freezer-burned inventory. The nights were getting a lot cooler and we packed up the tent for the year. Sedum were butterfly- and bee-covered, insects everywhere swirling up as much nectar as they could get. I tried not to think about the firefly guts and how long each may have lived.

And then, on a Friday, at recess, the school nurse huddled up with our old fifth-grade teacher and our new sixth-grade teacher. They all nodded, smiled, looked back at us at our picnic table, as we played the old card game my mom taught us called Gin Rummy.

All three walked over. I knew it had to be news of Cinta Johns, but I couldn't tell if their nods and smiles were good or bad. The regular sounds of the kickball being kicked and boys' cheers, the seesaw hee-hawing, the girls from The Slip singing jump rope songs, it all got way too loud, then fell to nothing. It was bad news. I just knew it. The school nurse said, "Your mom called, Lanie, to say that Cinta Johns is at the hospital." I set my cards down, didn't even care if the others saw my horrible, no-win hand. "They had to do a C-section, but she's doing fine and the baby is, too. One week early but perfectly healthy."

My knees buzzed. My heart nearly gave up. I tried my best not to cry, kept saying "broccoli" over and over, figuring if it could help keep me from sneezing, it could help keep me from doing the ugly bawl I'd been accustomed to lately right here at school. I couldn't believe it worked. We'd actually helped save Cinta Johns and her baby. Something bound to die had actually lived. I couldn't seem to move from my spot, but Tessa and Dawn jumped up and did our regular touchdown dance. Billie sat there staring at her playing cards. Lined up all four queens. Smiled.

There was no way I could stay at school, but my mom had likely imagined I'd say that and instructed that I was supposed to meet her at Cinta's house after school. We were picking up Sheppy and walking him to our house. He'd be staying with us for a few days.

All the words that came next from the teachers were a complete blur. But I caught, "Seven pounds. Six ounces. A little girl."

～

When we arrived at Cinta's house, Mom said, "I have arranged to take you girls to see the baby during visiting hours, when the curtains are open to the nursery."

"Will we get to see Cinta, too?" I asked. I had to make sure she was okay.

"Of course," Mom said.

I can't even say everything I felt standing there at the window, looking at that plexiglass holder where Cinta Johns's baby slept, Cinta's hands on my shoulders as warm as life could be. The baby's hands, fingers outstretched, reaching for whatever awesome and wonderful things life could hand her. "Lily," the name posted on the side in bright green letters, next to an even brighter bee. The nurse picked her up and brought her to the window. I swear the way she stared at each of us, she already knew us. She did.

"I can't ever thank you girls enough," Cinta said.

Mom jabbered with Tessa and Dawn and Billie the whole way home. I kept thinking about what a great name Lily would be and how Lily and Lanie sounded so perfect together.

The maples' leaves had started shifting to reds. The sun lit up the sky all shades of pink.

Nonna met us at the car, asked, "She so big? She cry loud?"

"Yes," my mom said. "She's a little angelo."

"Cinta use my necklace?"

"Yes," Mom said, and handed the bag to Nonna who pulled out the garlic necklace and placed it around her neck, its scent wafting through the evening air.

"Okay, good. Now, come come," Nonna said.

Soon we were plunging our hands in the dirt, not for the night crawlers we'd searched for so many months before as part of our fishing mission to feed Cinta Johns and her baby, but to plant the garlic Nonna had prepared for next year's crop, "Exactly four inches. No more. No less," Nonna said as she paced behind the four of us. She did know what the heck she was doing. That was for darn sure. I had to stand up and hug her. "All right, love you, too, chick-a-dee. Now getta back to work," she said.

We chattered about our sixth-grade teacher's huge bookcases and how we'd have to make some tea sachets for her, about how we'd have to help patch the roof on Mrs. Bianco's leaking henhouse, about how cool it would be to have Nonna teach us to tat matching bracelets for the four of us and Lily, and Cinta, too, about how young Sheppy seemed, sniffing the yard for squirrels, and we wondered if the mother possum finally let her baby off her back.

"Lightly, lightly," Nonna advised as we tucked into the ground each glowing, wonderful-smelling, beautiful garlic clove. "Lightly."

The cool garden soil felt amazing, sifting through our hands. The sounds of fall crept in where summer ones left off. But the crickets still sang to us, steady, sure.

Where Lottie Lived

Over the years, neighbors offered to buy Old Lottie Burns's house. She always said no. She'd die first before she'd ever let someone live in that house.

"What's her story?" she'd overheard people asking each other. Walking their dogs, they'd peer into her windows, checking to see if Lottie was still there. Never stopped to have a conversation with her, offer her a chance to tell her stories of the house.

She figured they just hoped to catch a glimpse of her long white hair, to see how bent she was, how she had to walk with her hands locked behind her, how she had to stare forever to the floor or the ground. At night kids corned her doors, soaped her windows, singing, "Lottie, Lottie, got a sweet body, drinks hot toddies, eats from her potty."

She ached to show them how beautifully she could sing, to tell them her father had cried once when she sang "Ave Maria."

After her father died, her mother and her priest had said, "Just let's hold onto the *good* memories. That's all we can do." And for the most part, she had.

Still, it was too much, this staying in the house alone. Too much to keep up. When her mother had finally passed—taking with her all the chances she had to say she was sorry, to explain why she'd turned her eyes away—Lottie allowed the house to rot. It didn't take long for skunks to make a home in the cellar, babies and all. Mice tenanted, gnawing sundry antechambers the length of the foundation.

One night she awakened to her father's words, "Damn hardheaded, you are." His voice had broken in. So she closed off those rooms where his sounds breathed from the switch plates, where his scent lingered in the floorboard knots. She no longer cared to cover with framed photos the plaster dents where the dog was slammed or where her skull connected. She took the frames down, picked at the wall's chalky pieces, let them fall to the floor.

Years passed and the Blessed Mother statue continued to heave from the ground roots, listing away from the house. A missing nose. Her blue gown chipped, mottled. Her eyes faded away—those same eyes Lottie once looked into while praying for intercession.

The night Lottie decided to leave the house for good, she'd been up late reading a book when two teenagers kicked over The Blessed Mother, laughing, running back to their remodeled homes up the street. The Blessed Mother lay there, helpless, on the ground.

Lottie willed her to get up.

Stand up.

But The Blessed Mother didn't move.

Yes, it was time to leave. The next day Lottie was gone. Where would she go? Anywhere but here. The lobby of the hospital, maybe the church's cry room, in that abandoned cabin out near the creek bed, in the Welles's pool house? There were so many places she could tuck in.

She settled into a warm spot behind the cheese shop, tried to make friends with the jittery strays.

The bus she rode daily to the mall routed past her once home and she peered from the window to watch the neighbor-man clearing out poison ivy and mayapples from around her house, as many of the weeds the spray could quit, to keep them from crossing the property line and into his space. He cut her hemlocks back, let light in.

Rhododendron burst again on the evening side of the house. Magenta. Stunning colors stirred without all those weeds strangling them out.

Then, without warning, he began filching the perennials. Dug for days. Quartered and transplanted clumps of Stella d'Oros, brown-eyed Susans, tiger lilies, sedum, wild phlox, daisies, hydrangeas, coneflowers, irises, peonies, bleeding hearts. He even dug up the rhododendron and hauled it to *his* evening side. All the faith of Lottie's mother's fingers now grew in another man's yard.

After he was sure his limp transplants rooted in, the neighbor-man let the weeds grow back in Lottie's yard.

A year later, the borough cited her, posting notes on the sunporch windows dotted by assaults of neighbor boys' BB guns. Code Offenses: High grass. Fire hazard.

The final warning came with a piece in the paper: *Raze the Eyesores!*

At the council meeting, folks claimed her house was the worst on their list, loud enough for her to hear as she sat staring straight ahead.

So many whispers.

Was it really her in the back row? She wanted to say, Yes, it's me, Lottie Burns.

She sensed no one could believe she'd shown up, that they were wondering, surely she wasn't there to pay those unpaid taxes and stop the Sheriff's sale? There was no Right of Redemption. They wanted at it. Yes. Wanted a chance to get inside that tight little house, get in that clutter and find what stories, or more, they could underneath all she'd hoarded there, what she'd left behind.

Over the years she'd heard everything they'd suspected. Might be silver squirreled in those walls—wasn't her mother's mother a collector? Might be cash nailed underneath those floorboards—didn't her father get a good pension from the mill? Might be bonds basted to the undersides of the mattresses—she'd started buying bonds when her father died in that mill accident, hadn't she?

In that meeting room, she sat there clutching a grocery bag full of clothes and the last of her money, nodding while they carped, jumping a little when the council president hit the gavel.

"They'll get in that house, doped-up punks," one council member warned. All heads bobbed.

Another added, "Old wiring. That house could explode!"

Lottie sniggered when he said that, picturing all the past explosions no one in the neighborhood ever cared to learn about: flung bottles of milk, dandelion wine, corn whiskey. She considered explaining but a man yelled out from the back of the room, voice booming, "Yeah, that damn wiring gotta be nibbled clean through by rats by now. Next thing you know we got ourselves a fire we can't put out."

She laughed a little thinking about how many times her father had threatened, "I'll burn you two to a crisp in this place," nearly touching his cigarette to the gauzy drapes as a warning.

Then a scent caught her. Something new in the meeting room. She raised her chin, sniffed, and found a memory tucked down deep. Her father's Bugler tobacco. He'd told her one evening—a pretty one like this, same lavender sky—how good she was at that task, "How perfect your little fingertips work, Lottie, rolling those cigs." He pursed his lips. She smiled and sprinkled more tobacco just so, rolled, careful not to rip anything, licked the paper.

That was before. She loved before. Before he'd taken her hand, told her to follow him.

But as soon as Lottie allowed that one happy memory to linger, another of her father's pet lines sprung out from a council member's tobacco-packed mouth, brown spittle at the creases of his lips: "Trouble's near. Fat's in the fire." The man closed his pouch of tobacco, hitched up his dungarees, and nodded with certainty just like her father had when he explained her mother would fuel the fire good with all her extra chub.

That's when she laughed and laughed until she couldn't breathe, until her ribs stung. That's when her bag toppled to the floor and people rushed to her, trying to reach their hands inside.

She threw her fists, connecting with one person's nose, another's lip. Blood sprayed.

She had withered to eighty-eight feisty pounds, about the same weight she was when she was held down the first time, when her mother went out to deadhead the roses neighbors had once slowed to see. Still, it took four councilmen to get her to the floor and hold her arms.

"Watch she don't hurt herself! Watch you don't hurt her!" a councilwoman yelled. Lottie's mother had said those same words from the hallway when Lottie's father closed the door behind them.

Lottie fought back. She held her legs closed, bit anything that came near her mouth. Then, when she knew she'd had enough, she pounded her head like she'd always done—one loud thump, just enough to bring her mother back in from the garden. This time it wasn't against the maple paneling of her bedroom wall, it was hard, again and again, against the cured concrete council-building floor. She felt her head come open like that muskmelon her father always promised her if she was good, if she just did what he said, just how he told her to do it. A good, sweet-smelling melon with gritty flesh.

Old Lottie died the next day in intensive care, purpled from struggle, strapped down to the last bed she'd have to suffer.

It sold, of course, the house. The bids, embarrassingly low. When the new owner got in, he searched for days but found nothing worth mentioning. No story worth telling in there.

Eminent Domain

*C*heezer worms up behind me, covers my eye sockets with his cold hands and breathes into my neck the word: "Guess."

He has something to tell and he loves rumor so much it makes him tremble; when he spreads it, his fingers always fiddle at his watery eyes, his watery lips. He always pulls at his cigarette, slows down, exhales, to make me wait. But tonight I know the story. Still, I'll let him tell it to me like it's new because I know how the telling drops his clothes off quicker.

But let me put it to you so you know it right.

My pap—in the midst of all his talk about shifting power grids, the high and low voltage, about Marcellus shale, the dry and wet gas—mentioned they were going to rebuild the substation and made promises to replace and raise all those wood poles clean from Toby Furnace to Bennett's Corners. But no matter how high you string those wires above the ground, a body still feels the prickly snap underneath them. Like mom's little cuticle scissors nipping at my skin. First time I walked there I thought sure bugs were biting at my ankles. I mean I swore it. Checked my skin for red bites. Fire ants threading my hairs off. But nothing. And the grass was extra slippy, even when it wasn't damp.

We'd take guys out there through that grass to the shed, to party, to forget we were stuck.

The shed was smack dab under the power lines. We had some good times there, I'm telling you. The guys chirping like goslings, talking about shooting up whitetails, trapping bunnies, fishing monster trout at the Sidle, lifting the bodies of their Fords and Chevys, until we filled their mouths with Henny and Red Bull. After a few, they always swayed their words out, got quiet and cuddly. Whispery and soft. But then some Suit from the company put up a No Trespassing sign and we moved our party to the old baseball dugouts for a while.

Then we got kicked out of there, too.

The shed's now a crime scene and we lost our spot. Someone's been killing cats and storing them in there. Cats. Sharkie Smail's ex-con uncle said there was over two hundred in there.

I know the guy who's doing the killing and I know why. Pap told me when he was lit on homemade pruno Sharkie's uncle taught him to make.

This guy doing it thinks the cats are the devil.

This place can do that to you. I've seen it do worse to smart people.

≈

Cheezer pulls his hands away and says, "Cats strung on lines, gutted, little wilting whiskers all pointing straight to Hell. Can you believe it? Don't it just make you sick? Don't it just break your heart?"

I nod and kiss his neck. I feel how warm he is in certain places and he says, "Who you think could do that?"

"No idea," I say. It's always better to keep him pondering something when we get to it. And when we're done and he's tugging his jeans back on and I'm worrying he just shot something that might grow up in me, I have other things to mull over, too. Because as much as he's nice and handsome in a lonely kind of way and I can picture staying here and having a life, I know I have to hop in my car and drive far as I can get if I want to ever be anything that ain't a few steps away from crazy.

Loosed

*I*t was a pity how they found Luke, all bloodied up, banging his head on a wood and wire cage near his old pits. Thrust from the weeds there. He'd been strutting around like one of his old fighting cocks, elbows winging out at the sides.

When they tried to restrain him, get him into the cruiser, then the ambulance, he kept jerking away, making signals with his hands, kept mumbling numbers, names. "Luke Jr., Sammy, Baby, Seckel." At the ER, they sedated him. He was out for hours, though still twitching, fingers trying to dance out some sign.

People from the city who'd recently moved upriver to build modest summer places with retirement savings from their engineering jobs at Westinghouse, US Steel, PPG, and Kennametal had been complaining about Luke's snooping around their camps, squawking like a bird, scaring their grandchildren.

He'd likely returned to the pits in Pope because it was all he knew. The site of his first blood business.

The Spot—that's what everyone called it—was about ten miles from the center of town where the river doglegged back to a dark piece wooded in heavy cover. At one point he had over a hundred roosters at The Spot tethered on short lines to keep them angry. Every Saturday night people came to bet on them, to hear Luke brag about his fine Miner Blues, his sturdy Roundheads, his wicked Madigin Clarets and White Hackles. All tough and mean and best in the state. He walked around with his star bird, Abe, sticking its face up to the caged fighters to get them roused up, saying, "Gonna be good fights tonight. Gonna be schooled!"

~

Luke Abraham was a small man in position, stature, and intelligence. He stood at five foot six, though his crew cut of red hair gained him another inch. After quitting school, end of the ninth grade, he worked as a caddy at the country club, peddled an egg route, and shined shoes on Market Street to help his widowed mother keep their home from the bank. He thought he might meet the girl he'd marry while in Centerville, across the bridge working his egg route, but the wealthy girls there ignored him, waved him away. The summer Luke's mother passed and he turned twenty-seven, one girl, June, who ran the register at the sandwich shop, showed some interest in him. She was only sixteen but had no parents to say no, so she and Luke eloped, ran across the border to Winchester, came back to town in three days, married. She was sick already with his first son, just beginning to show.

Back then, more than anything, he wanted sons, sons who would be somebody more than him, who would become doctors or engineers, lawyers or senators. As if the universe had answered his wish, his wife quickly had four boys. Luke couldn't have been more thrilled.

When the last one was born, Luke cut back to a handful of laying chickens, stopped shining altogether. He told his wife, "No father of no boys should be peddling eggs or spit-shining shoes, no matter how good the tips are," and that's when he got the idea to start raising gamecocks to bring in a little extra cash.

Cockfighting had been a middling business for Luke. People who showed had little to wager—stuck in low-income, go-nowhere jobs. Luke himself brought in only slim wages with his work as a part-time mechanic and carpenter. He repaired boat engines throughout the summer at the marina, sometimes took payment in cases of Rolling Rock beer. He did small additions, some roofing, but more established contractors in the area grabbed most of that work. Still, he could use that steady trickle of money from these cross birds to better feed and clothe his children. That was the deal he made with his young wife. She wouldn't ask questions about splattered blood she cleaned from his clothes, and he'd continue to bring in enough money to raise the kids above the poverty line. However, because she hated the sounds of the cocks screaming out—"a God-awful sound, Luke!"—he promised to keep his business far enough away from their home so she didn't have to hear how that money was raised. That's when he stumbled upon the place in Pope, and he squatted his whole business there.

But by the time the youngest boy was five, they needed more money.

Dogs, Luke soon found, brought more profits. So he slaughtered the birds and bred pit bull terriers.

Businessmen from the city started to venture up the river to bet. Big business. Suits. Guys who'd heard about the dogs from traveling through and selling products to the owners of the local lumberyards, hardware and paint stores. These Suits, these salesmen with their big expense accounts, seemed to have more than enough money to bet on the dogs. They also paid Luke to tinker on their boats, fix things that weren't really broken yet. Now, rather than rely only on venison, Luke could buy enough beef to keep all winter. He could buy ample milk for four growing boys, enough milk to soak trout in all day before he grilled, enough to spill.

It was all good.

He was meeting men of such stock and position he never thought possible.

Within two years the dog business was real solid. So solid, in fact, Luke could finally purchase that twenty-four-foot Sea Ray sport boat he'd always dreamed of having. June wasn't happy, but she asked if he'd at least name it after her. Instead, Luke christened it Lucullus after the nickname one of these bettors—a man everyone referred to as Doc—gave him. Some said Doc was a professor of history at one of the city colleges. To be nicknamed by him was an honor, Luke assured his wife.

"An honor?" his wife asked and scrunched up her nose, then rubbed it in that way that once entertained Luke but now annoyed the hell out of him.

"Yes. He said Lucullus was this Roman *elite*, you know, who had these big feasts and pitted dogs, too. Like me."

She tapped a cig out of her pack, lit it. "That right?"

"Yes, Juney, that's right," he said, polishing the boat with his chamois.

Still, he went to the library one afternoon, had the librarian look up Lucullus to make sure the nickname wasn't an insult as so many he'd been tagged with had been.

"Oh, yes, he was famous," the young librarian said as she ran her finger over the block of text Luke could mostly read.

With the newer clientele, the worry of fines and aggravation he'd suffered during his cockfighting days simply disappeared, though he was warned that could all change if he got reckless.

"Keep a little more quiet, Luke," one state boy said when he showed up in his unmarked car. He had some sort of connection with one of the men from the city—not a salesman, but a Suit with serious political connections. "Don't want just anyone showing up, right?" He looked past the rape stands and the ropes and small animal carcasses Luke used in forced exhaustion exercises.

The state boy came the next month, too, hunched down to take a closer look at the cage of wild rabbits the beagle club up the road had sold to Luke for training purposes. He reached in to pet the timid silvery-brindle animals as he talked. Luke offered him a ring of deer bologna and a bottle of homemade dandelion wine as a gesture of goodwill—one of the rabbits, too, if he wanted. The state boy winked, tried to wipe the downy fur from his fingers onto his black polyester uniform pants, grabbed the bottle and ring, and left.

Luke got another friendly visit three months later. It was just after Luke had shown up at an overrun animal shelter two counties away with his oldest boy, had taken four unwanted mutts off their hands for what he promised would be a good life of roaming free in a pasture just playing with his four boys. Instead, he used them as bait animals. The state boy said, "People would rather know the shelter was gassing them dogs than to think about how you're using them. Come on, Luke. Cut that shit out." He shook his head. "Word like that gets out we'll have Animal Control up our asses."

But for the most part, cops stayed away.

With this freedom from the law officially butting in, Luke had facilitated more canine fighting, and subsequently more terrier breeding, than anyone in three counties, maybe the state, by the time his oldest boy, Luke Jr., was almost twelve.

Luke was set. Not set like the wealthy in town, but not hurting either.

And he hadn't even hit forty years old yet.

But his wife met him at the door one night just after the best take he'd had at The Spot, blowing out a question into her exhaled smoke, "Can't you just be done with this?" She took in another drag, then added, "You know, get a respectable job at the mill, Luke?"

"Why the hell would I do that?" He took a long look at her face through the cloud she'd made between them. When he'd met her at sixteen, she looked nearly twenty—all painted up with makeup to send her eyes into striking sideways glances, her glossed lips soft, smoking those Benson & Hedges like she was old enough to. Now, after giving birth to the four boys and sucking down two, sometimes three packs a day for years, she looked nearer Luke's age, maybe older, with those makeup-caked lines around her lips and her eyes and her bunched-up, nitpicking forehead.

She kept it coming. "It's not right, the boys seeing all that with those dogs growling and biting and—"

"Those dogs are what gives you your fancy hairdos and clothes. You keep your mind to yourself."

The next week when one of the dogs snagged Sam's forearm, she said, "Now how am I to explain this to the doctor?"

"I'll get it taken care of. Jesus. Kids get bit all the time."

But she threw her cigarette to the floor. When Luke yelled, "Hey, hey, hey," she smashed it with her shoe, blowing smoke from the side of her mouth.

After she returned home from the ER and put Sam to bed, reading to him until he calmed down and could sleep, she came into the kitchen all shaking hands and whispering worry. He sat at the table, wordless, while she wrote down the antibiotic schedule and went over the ways they had to deal with the wound. "Are you listening to any of this?" she asked.

"Yes."

That's when she started up her complaining about the fights, saying that he had to focus more on the boys, how this was messing with them, how this would maim them with worse than bites.

Luke said, "You don't like how I'm providing here, you can just leave."

And she did.

When Luke came home late the following night, he found the house dark, the old Plymouth Sport Fury gone. He stared at the oil stains on the concrete floor for a few minutes before he went back to the bedroom to find her clothes and suitcase gone. She left a note propped up on the only wedding photo they had—a snapshot of them leaning against the Fury, her in a white sundress and him in a short-sleeved yellow dress shirt and new pleated pants.

> Don't know the first thing about how to keep a
> woman happy.

Find out now what it's like to take care of a
house yourself.
Don't you dare let Sam's wound get infected.
Won't be back until the dogs are gone. Headed
to May's.
Boys are welcome to join me if they care to.

Luke knew she'd be back, especially with Sam's condition. But he
did check the freezer, saw she took a couple thousand from the bag
of peas where he kept his cash.

Just before dawn, Luke got the call from the sheriff's deputy
who'd found the car nearly flattened to nothing. On the way to her
sister's, June had hit head-on with a southbound coal truck on the
first run, sending that blood money to stick itself in the bitterweed
and chicory of the berm and median, parts of her chubby, twenty-
eight-year-old body embedded into the dash.

The truck driver called Luke personally to say he stood on
those brakes, laying a patch of rubber so thick it could be seen from
the moon. "Not a damn thing I coulda done different. I turned it
over in my head."

Luke shook his head at the words, hung up the phone without
saying goodbye, and drove straight to the barracks to see the trooper
who'd been on the scene first, just to hear his account again, in
person. He patted Luke's shoulder, repeated several times that they
had no reason to believe she hadn't just nodded off or got distracted
lighting up a cig. Luke lifted his chin and left.

Two days later, the four boys—his oldest, Luke Jr., the twins,
Sammy and Baby Boyd, and the youngest, Galen, nicknamed Seckel
the day he was born for the birthmark on his cheek shaped like a
pink Seckel pear—all stood tall flanking the casket, holding their

jaws steady. They shook hands of visitors, some bettors from the pits, some ladies from the church Luke's wife occasionally attended, and silently nodded to each "Be strong now" and "I'm so sorry for your loss" and "You help your daddy." When it was time to load that closed casket into the hearse, Luke motioned for the boys to go along with the undertaker.

He pumped up his chest when he saw all four of them holding onto the rails of that casket, easing it—with the help of a few of Luke's buddies from the pit—into the back of the hearse, bending a little under the weight of her. A few grievers leaned in, said, "So big they're getting," "So proud you must be," and he was. In the midst of what should have felt like a great loss, he couldn't help but smile when he saw how many flowers the bettors had sent, that the big shot boss at the mill had sent the largest spray. He told the boys that meant they were important, too. Luke made a promise to them and to himself that he'd steer the boys to that kind of success one day. Or better. Whatever it took.

~

He threw himself deeper into the business after June passed. What else could he do? He kept the boys busy, refused to talk about what wasn't, and made them focus on what was. What was, was opportunity for all of them. What was, was some damn good luck.

Over the next two years, more and more men arrived to bet on dogs with more and more money. The number of prominent people showing up at The Spot increased. And these men were all so delighted to finally meet Luke. They patted him on the back, shook his hand hard with folded hush bills as they arrived, even though they never gave their real names.

Luke did everything in his power to keep his business respectable. The conditioning devices, spring poles, and breeding boxes were housed at the far end of the site. Paths to the pits were free of mud puddles, for Luke had the boys spread limestone in the low spots before each fight. He had them string more lights along the path from the dock.

The boys helped with the training and bathing the inevitable topical drug here or there from the coats of the fighters. They had a checklist to complete, were good about staying out of the way once betting started, never talked unless Luke gave them permission. In fact, he taught the boys signals for each of their tasks: a wink when a dog's jaw locked in and he was ready for the break stick to release it, a finger snap when he wanted them to redraw chalked lines in the pit.

He gripped his wrist, held up two fingers when a dog showed weakness. At this signal, the boys walked away from the pit and the cheering straight to the shed to gather up the sack, bricks, the rope or the gun, always the shovel, and they waited, as Luke instructed them, for the gentlemen bettors to leave before they brought the supplies back to the pit.

After the last bettor walked off, the last boat left, Luke strolled past the battered and bloody fighters—his four boys in tow—pointing to the dogs to keep around for another fight, holding up two fingers for the ones he wanted destroyed. Sometimes he grabbed the gun and just offed a dog himself. Once, his anger so great at the losses, he kicked a dog to death. Another time he grabbed the rope, hung one of the dogs from a tree. "See here. See what you get if you don't fight good and hard?" he yelled out to the cowering dogs. "See?" He turned back to the boys. "Damn it, get your goddamned hands off your eyes, Sam!"

Most times, though, he'd just give that two-finger signal and walk off, leaving Luke Jr. to do away with the dogs, usually with some help from Seckel, who looked up to his brother in all ways. Together they'd figured out a way they could lure the maimed dog into the sack with some kibble, knew how long to wait after the bubbles rose up from the water to pull the sack up and find the body matted down with the river water that had washed most of the blood clean. Bury it proper in the loamy soil.

After a few times they did it that way, Luke said, "Use enough bricks, it'll stay put for the carp to eat up."

"But Dad, them dog ears keep coming into my dreams, floating along the water," Seckel said, scratching his forearm, staring at the ground.

"Suit yourself," Luke said, shaking out his hands and walking away.

～

How did it turn? At first it happened by accident that his twins got into a scrap outside the pit when two bull terriers were fighting. But during the dogfight, some of the men were not looking for snatch in the pit; they were preoccupied with the boys, with their tussled hair, dust kicked up onto their sinewy bodies, blood and dirt at their mouths, the look of something not quite known.

When Luke noticed how excited these men got watching the boys fight, he played around with an idea. It helped, too, that this same idea was suggested by one of the heavy bettors, Doc, who'd said, "Now you have something worth looking at here, Luke."

That's when Luke decided to pit the boys against each other. Bare-knuckle.

"Will people bet on that?" Luke asked around.

"Absolutely." "Sure." "Oh, damn. Yes."

As soon as word leached out about a man who put boys, his own young sons, in the pit to fight, that rumor spread through a series of channels, deeper and more dangerous than the ones that drowned good river swimmers, through strata blacker than the minerals that brought and bred money in the town. Word came to them through the surgeon at the local hospital—same one who'd set his sons' bones or stitched up wounds quietly at Luke's own home. They found out through the judge himself, a peculiar man Luke knew fancied anything nubile. They found out through the bankers. Then finally they found out through local old money who'd started paying more attention to Luke.

Some men who rolled in to see Luke's four sons fight, who traveled up and down the river and deep into the wood, came there from a different set altogether, had a steady flow of money, power. But they weren't just rich. "Seem to be smart, decent human beings," Luke said about these witty, white-haired men, some who wiped their noses with silk hankies, wore perfumed pastel golf shirts, others who smoked Cuban cigars, wore ivory cufflinks. Still more who were Bohemian, wide-browed, brought him books, plants. They fascinated him. Two of them—a religious scholar of some sort and a bigwig lawyer for one of the city banks—spent hours arguing over whether the line on the sign at the pit, "What counts is not the size of the dog in the fight but the size of the fight in the dog," was a chiasmus or an antimetabole.

"It's just a quote. By a writer. Mark Twain," Luke said. "And Ike said it, too." Luke thought he had settled it. He felt sure he had impressed them when they smiled back at him.

These men were otherworldly.

Luke wanted, more than anything, to stir them, to have their eyes on him and his boys.

The first few fights proved the prize Luke had bred, how lucrative it would be to use his own blood to make money. These enigmatic men stood nearer to Luke, whispering in his ear, slipping him an extra five or ten or twenty, their aftershave wafting away the smell of the fishy river. And the boys, they looked to their dad for pointers and signals as they fought over and over again. He'd rub his hand across his forearm, tip his hat, do some strange whip of his wrist. Immediately the boys did what he asked. He melted into a sort of dance when one of the boys took a dive at just the right time to assure the winnings and losses were on mark. These little dances intrigued the men. "What are you telling them with the way you move like that, Luke, with those signals?" one bettor asked early on.

Luke smiled, quickly replied, "You know, they're young. Gotta remind them to save up their energy, to breathe, you know? They forget their combos. Hell, half the time, they forget to look to me."

The bettor laughed, shaking Luke's hand.

But Luke knew the boys were tuned in. They practiced the signals as much as their jabs.

The business was tight, thriving. He started training the boys much the same way he'd trained the dogs. Forced them to exercise until they had dry heaves. Slapped them around to get them started.

June's sister, May, called twice, asking about them, had heard something she wasn't sure she believed about the boys fighting. Luke lied. He lied so good, she believed him.

⌇

Midsummer, Luke scheduled a fight between the twins. No dogs fought that night. Just the boys. More men attended than could fit around the pit, three rows thick. Luke offered a spread of wild game and fish: blackened trout he'd tricked from the Sidle, buttered walleye he'd caught upriver from The Spot, stuffed bear meat shells in a Roma sauce his mother had taught him to make, fresh fried venison loin, roasted quail in a sour cherry and wild mushroom sauce.

Oh, there was more money than had ever been offered up when the dogs fought.

It was a long and tedious scrap. Neither wanted to give up. Only command Luke gave them: "Fight hard."

The weak twin won. Boyd. Luke and his boys had always called him Baby. He had the face of a girl, long curled eyelashes, sweet hazel eyes, blond hair strung in rings when wetted by the heat of the humid summer air and dusk-to-dawn lights of the muddied pit.

Luke whispered promises to Luke Jr.—for he was the one who couldn't understand why they had to fight, why they couldn't just go back to only dogs—listing all the things he'd buy them if they just kept fighting like this.

"How 'bout that Browning you've been eyeing up at—"

"I got a good rifle, Dad."

"What about that YZ85 out there in the showroom at Kibuk's? You could jump anything you want on that there bike." Luke punched his son's shoulder. "Come on, now."

Luke Jr. pursed his lips and nodded.

"Baby won," said one of the men a few feet from Luke and Luke Jr.

"No shit."

"I'm telling you, he did." The men were all whoops and hollers.

"See that?" Luke said to Luke Jr. "Did you hear that? We surprised them. That's how we make money."

"But do we each get wins or what?"

"We'll see what happens."

The strong twin, Sam, had scrapes and was purpled up here and there. "I'm sorry, I'm sorry, I'm sorry," he echoed as he lay there on the dusty ground while Luke paid off the bets. Sam was used to winning.

Luke explained to Sam in the quiet of the wood out behind the pit, "Losing got you more this time, Sam. You did right."

"But Dad—"

"I said, you did right."

The surgeon, who took the biggest cut of the pot, treated Baby Boyd afterward for dehydration.

"That'll be free of charge, right?" Luke whispered.

"Of course, Luke," the surgeon replied with a wink.

Seckel, the youngest, had just turned ten at the time of that fight. After watching the fight between Sam and Baby Boyd—how long it had gone on, how much blood spilled—he begged his dad not to make him punch his brothers when it was his turn. He went to Luke each day, tried to make a deal. "Please, Dad? I know I can fight, I don't mind gettin' mean and all that, but I don't like that sufferin' blood. Makes my stomach flip, Dad. Whatever else you want, I'll do."

"Now, I know you don't like it, but you're gonna do it. You are the bravest of all you boys." Seckel could hold a shotgun to the head of a battered terrier after a fight gone bad—even pull the trigger—but it was true about the suffering blood. He couldn't bear to see fresh blood coming from anything living. He was the one who had it the worst when June was killed, kept waking in the night, asking how much she might have bled from the impact of that coal truck, how long she might have bled before she died. Luke figured the only reason Seckel could pull a trigger was because it assured him the blood on the dogs would eventually stop.

As promised, though, to his loyal customers, Luke put Seckel in the pit with Baby Boyd. He'd told Seckel no hitting, just wrestle and bite. The men cheered at the sight of the two boys locked in a hold, one with his teeth set into the shoulder of the other. And while Seckel hated the sight of blood, he told his dad after the fight that, paired with all those cheers, all them eyes on him, all them high-fives, and smiles, well, the taste of the blood of his brothers was good. Soon, the men took the nickname Luke had given the boy for the Seckel pear birthmark to mean something else entirely. They called him Sickle, like the blade, because he was the one, ever after, who always drew blood.

Luke extended the fighting into October that year—alternating between dog fights and boy fights each weekend. He talked to one of the men about putting up a pole building for fighting all winter, started making sketches.

On Sundays he took the boys out on the boat, sending them into giggling fits when he hopped it over wakes of larger boats. One cloudy Sunday, mid-October, they headed to the cove. "Bass'll come outta hiding when it clouds up nice like this," Luke yelled over the motor to the boys. They nodded and smiled, their long bangs whipping into their eyes. But when they got there, motored down, went to drop anchor, somehow the light punched through those thick clouds and laid a patch onto Seckel's face, shining into the purple, yellow, and tint of green that flanked his swollen left eye.

Luke was unable to look away. Tiny freckles blended the old and new bruises. Seckel's nose had grown wider, but the yellowed bridge of it showed what made it flatten that way. And something about the scar below it, where a future mustache might be, seemed to distort the boy's upper lip, leaving a bead of flesh where Luke now realized nothing would grow. Sam stepped between Luke and Seckel, asking a question about bait, and Luke answered, staring now at Sam's chest—the brush burns across the upper right side. Just below those burns there was a knot of purple that looked like it might explode if Luke touched it. He was both in awe and sickened by how many hits and licks their bodies had taken. But, when he saw Luke Jr. lift his T-shirt over his head, exposing the injuries he'd gotten the night before, he quickly turned away, busying himself with fishing gear.

When Baby Boyd got stuck with a hook—"Sorry, Dad, sorry!"—and a single drop of blood rose out of the end of his tiny finger, Luke shook his head and yelled out, "Hell with this. We won't catch nothing now that the sun's out. Let's take a swim instead."

He downed his Rolling Rock and jumped over the side of the boat.

The boys hesitated at first.

Luke Jr. asked, "Ain't it too cold? Won't we freeze?"

"Hell no. What are ya? Sissies?" Luke flapped his arms. "Woo-hoo! Reee-freshing!"

The boys kicked off their shoes and cannonballed off the side of the boat, repeating, when they came up for air, "Reee-freshing."

Life couldn't have been better than that. To see those boys' heads bobbing in this river that would someday take them wherever they wanted to go.

On the way back upriver, he instructed them to just keep telling anyone who asked that they got bungled up in a pick-up tackle game at home or that they wrecked their four-wheelers.

"Don't worry, Miss P. believed me, Dad," Sam said.

"Well, good. That's good. Ain't none of their business anyhow, but they're bound to ask."

Sam smiled.

~

A few men from the lower end of Centerville needed money after one of the mines closed and offered their sons up, too, for cash, but the boys were too scared, made fools of themselves in the training. The junior-high wrestling coach from the next town over paid a visit late one night, made a deal with Luke, but he backed out at the last minute, afraid some parent might have a change of heart and decide to call the teacher's union. He passed on the name and number of the juvie schoolmaster, though, and suddenly Luke had more than enough boys to pick from to go up against his sons.

In November, cold weather set in and kept the boats and cars away. Again, Luke trained his sons constantly, often sending them into crying fits. He loaded them up with venison, and when each could take a punch to the gut without wincing, he finally bought them the game consoles he'd promised them months before.

When early spring blew in, life in the pit came back. The boats crawled back upriver, dodging driftwood and shining with promise. Luke stood on his tiptoes on the open bow of his Sea Ray waving them into the newly planked three-finger u-docks.

Luke Jr., now a muscular fourteen and a fan favorite from the summer before, would have brought the biggest crowds all summer.

However, after he knocked out Baby, who'd just turned twelve, in the opening night fight, he ran away to his aunt May's home in Ohio. He hitchhiked the whole way there, then called Luke, whispering—through the wobble and static of his changing voice and the bad connection—that he'd never be back.

"But Lukie, listen to me." Luke cleared his throat. "Your brothers need you here." Luke could hear his son's sobbing. "Come on, now. *I* need you here."

"Dad, I just can't do it no more, I—"

"Now you listen. This is how I get you boys somewhere, you see? This is how we get noticed."

"Dad, I—"

"You what? Don't you want to be somebody?"

"Yeah, but—"

"Then you get back here."

The line went dead. Luke stared at the phone for a long time before he set it down, thrummed his fingers on the table. Then he waited, floating his palms over the nicks in its surface. Seckel walked into the kitchen and Luke held up a hand. "Get to bed. Nothing out here concerns you," Luke said.

Seckel nodded, turned away.

Luke thrummed again. He was sure Luke Jr. would call back asking for someone to come fetch him at May's as soon as he realized how good he was in the pit. He was a strong, scrappy fighter who put his all into each and every fight. Luke knew how much the crowds loved his ginger-haired boy, loved his fiery temper in the pit when provoked by the men calling him Red and by his brothers laughing right along with the men.

But Luke Jr. never called back. Not that night. Not ever.

Luke Jr.'s absence put significant pressure on the twins and Seckel to fight more often. This fighting went on for that whole summer and well into the fall again. Luke thought the boys from the juvie center would make up for the loss of Luke Jr., but those boys hadn't been trained like Luke's sons. The knockouts were swift. On the other hand, the fights between Luke's sons brought more electricity to the pit. They lasted longer and yielded more wagers. There was something different about siblings fighting than random boys fighting, something about watching Luke coach them to strike and maim each other. It went to the core of these men and swelled their bets.

Over the course of the summer, the tough twin, Sam, got chubby. Seckel, who'd been pummeled by him the summer before, could now easily knock him out. The crowd became a chorus of gaping mouths and back-slapping insults. "Get that piggy on his back, now, Sickle," one man with slicked black hair said—everyone was calling him Sickle now. "He won't get up. He can't!" So Sam threatened to run away like his brother, and Luke decided to pay the boys a cut of the profit, spoiling them with new dirt bikes, four-wheelers. The boys fought harder and longer, made their father more money than he could have imagined.

But that's when Baby Boyd got slow—not just in fighting but in speaking, thinking, in everything. He'd had his bell rung damn hard more times than Luke could keep track of, but Luke kept fighting him because he was always the wild card. Once he got a taste of winning, he went all out.

The last fight ever came in late September when the nights were starting to cool, sending the crickets scraping into a slow bluesy tune.

After the juvie boys fought the first two matches, and the dogs the next three, the twins were scheduled to fight. Sickle, who was favored, would fight the winner of that round.

The crowd buzzed right along with the dusk-to-dawn lights. Men swooped here and there, flapping money overhead like the wings of bats.

Luke watched as the twins exploded in the pit. Dust flew, fists thudded, blood sprayed.

Little Sickle watched, too, bouncing at first next to Luke and then calming, like Luke, into a stare.

The crowd wanted Sam to win because they couldn't wait to see Sickle take him out in the second round of fighting.

But the fight went long.

The moon sank low and bloody. Luke looked away from the pit, eyeing first the moon and then the crowd. He stared into the faces of each bettor, but no one returned his gaze. He paced around the perimeter, whispering to himself. Then he walked back to Sickle. He looked him over. The kid was well under five feet tall, freckles all over his face, arms, back. He leaned down to level Sickle with his own eyes, whispered, "No matter who wins this one, you'll dive."

Sickle shook his head, pointed to the pit, then made his fists tight and pounded them against his thighs.

Luke raised his brows. "You'll dive, I said."

Luke stood up straight again, took in a deep breath, and walked back to the pit. Just then Baby Boyd started laughing. He let Sam pound him. The crowd cheered. Baby's face snapped left, right, left, right, and he giggled, spit out blood, a few teeth, stood longer.

Sam stopped hitting for a moment and looked to his father in disbelief. This wasn't how it was supposed to go. Sam was supposed to let his slow twin take him down, wrestle him to the ground. Sam was supposed to take kicks to the side, get up, then start hitting harder. Sam was supposed to look to his father for the sign. But now he only stared at his twin. Enraged at Baby, mistaking his dim-witted laughter for ridicule, Sam suddenly went all out. Despite his father's order to let Baby win, Sam threw his brother down to the ground and beat his head, again and again, into the dusty earth.

"Look at me!" Luke screamed, exaggerating the gestures he usually disguised. But it was too late.

Some men in the crowd murmured the word for the first time: "Setup."

Luke jumped in, tried to split them up.

"Dad, Dad, don't stop him!" Sickle cried from the side, panicking, looking around at the scowling crowd. "They want to see them fight, Dad. Let them go."

"What's wrong, Daddy?" The slow twin, Baby Boyd, raised his bloodied brows and peered at his father quizzically through two purple swollen eyes. Luke turned, then, to the crowd, and kicked at the wall of the pit, threatening with his fists held high, "Get out, get out of here, all of you. Go. Get out!"

Sickle jumped into the pit with his father and brothers and tried to pull his father's arms down. "Stop, Dad!"

Luke rounded up the boys and tried to hold them there in the short span of his arms.

Some men made threats. Some shook their heads.

One unbuckled his hip snap, cocked the hammer, and held his .44 Magnum Desert Eagle to Luke's head, demanding his money from all the fights. Light from the dusk-to-dawn reflected off that titanium gold barrel. The boys' whimpering blended with the crickets' and cicadas' cries, the screeching of the docks as they rose and fell from their poles and cable tethers.

"Hey man, come on," said another bettor, walking closer to the man with the gun. Then two more talked him down, pulled the gun away, saying it wasn't worth it. They all just took their money, walked toward the river.

Sam and Sickle peeled themselves from Luke and ran from the pit, Sickle yelling out to the last of the men from the bow of his father's boat what Luke would always say after the fights, "Come back next week, now! Come back. Hey, be sure to come back!"

Luke laid Baby Boyd on the dusty ground of the pit, gave him the signal to rest. Baby smiled at him, his eyes swollen, the skin beneath them split and bleeding. "How'd I do?"

~

Luke knew it was all over. He opened the pens and let the dogs go. The ones who were too fearful to leave, cowering in the backs of their pens, he shot and buried before the authorities came.

He made up some complicated story about the boys wrecking their four-wheeler, not wearing their helmets, then changed it to say a big-screen TV fell on Baby, right on his face. Swore they were messing around in the living room and it fell.

"Listen, Luke, just stop," the state boy said, pointing back to the one unmarked vehicle of the four that showed up at The Spot, the one without the flashing lights. A minivan with a logo on the door—CYS: Children and Youth Services. "We have no choice here. The call came from your sister-in-law, May Wynkoop, from Ohio?"

Luke let them cuff him. He let them load him into the cruiser.

The state took the boys. Put them in foster care. Wouldn't let May take them because her husband had a DUI. But somehow Luke Jr. was allowed to stay on with her.

After his six months in county, probation for two more, Luke sort of went underground, like he had never even existed.

Everyone thought the boys would end up on drugs or dead but they turned out okay.

"They can't be right after that," people who knew about the fighting said, but Baby Boyd grew up fine, got a job at the recycling center sorting plastic from cans. Everyone loved to see him each week. He knew everyone's names. He was happy to take the bags and boxes from their cars and trucks, smiling, whistling, giving high-fives to all who stopped by.

Sam's foster father was a gym teacher. He took him to the YMCA every day to train. Sam slimmed down, broke some records as a three-sport athlete. He made his body into a sculpture of sorts. After high school, he landed a full-time job at the mines, running a roof-bolter, doing his best to keep his fellow miners safe.

Sickle moved from home to home until he turned eighteen, then worked his way from stock boy to assistant manager at a box store, and the oldest boy, Luke Jr., who ran away to Ohio when he was fourteen, went on to college and secured a nice job as a staff writer for a newspaper in Cincinnati.

∿

Luke finally came to but soon had to be restrained to the hospital bed due to his scratching and pawing at his skin. His voice was raspy as he continued to whisper the boys' names. "We found them.

They're on their way. All of them," the social worker said, squeezing Luke's hand. "Don't worry."

Luke lifted his head from the pillow, straining his neck to see through the thin window of the door, widening his eyes and smiling, so much that his dry lips split.

"We'll bring them to you," the social worker said. "Just rest now. Just rest."

"Okay," Luke said, tears leaking from his eyes.

Sam was the first to arrive. He'd been called out from under the hill just after his shift started and heard from his former foster father what had happened to Luke. Sickle wasn't far behind; he met Sam in the parking lot and they took a smoke before entering the ER, talked about how hot the summer had been.

A social worker headed them off at the waiting room, explaining how poor their father looked, trying to prepare them for what they'd see. "He's a little confused, but he was happy to know you're coming." She offered to buy them dinner at the snack bar while Luke was having some tests. She handed each her card, told them Luke had been living in his old boat on the river. He was dehydrated and very weak, may have had a ministroke. After they ordered their food, she said she felt their father should be committed, gave them each a pamphlet to read over. She kept asking, "Do you have any questions?" They shook their heads.

When they returned to the waiting room, Baby Boyd arrived, smiles and hugs for all, including the social worker.

"So are you ready to go in, then?"

"We can't make any decisions until Luke Jr. gets here," Sickle said, his voice cutting out. "I—I think we should just wait to see him when everyone's here."

"Understood," she said. "We can wait for your brother. Your father needs to rest now anyway."

They sat in the waiting room, Baby asking questions every so often and humming, Sam answering some but mostly silent, leafing through magazines, and Sickle staring at the TV.

Luke Jr. didn't arrive until dark, just as the sheriff's deputy showed up to read off the list of charges. He said Luke had likely survived on dog food and the eggs from the one laying hen he kept on the boat with him. They'd also found a dead dog on the boat, maybe one leftover from Luke's original brood. There was a rumor that he'd continued breeding, but no one had confirmed that.

"It had mange too," the deputy said, shaking his head.

"Wait. Dad has mange?" Sam asked.

The social worker chimed in, "Yes, well, scabies."

"We're ready to sign," Luke Jr. said, wiping his hands on his jeans.

"Okay, we'll get him processed then, and you can see him upstairs in 2A in about fifteen minutes."

Baby Boyd giggled when the security guard patted them down at the entrance of the psych ward. All four boys filed in as the social worker went over the visiting hours and procedures.

Luke nodded to them as they came in. He sat there in the bed, swimming in the oversized olive scrubs. While the social worker continued to talk, Luke listened, scratching at his waist and the nape of his neck. He nodded and mumbled nonsense words to himself. His red hair had turned white and his face and forearms were covered in scabs, but he was clean-shaven and his eyes sparkled. He seemed to recognize them. When he opened his mouth, he couldn't make words come.

Sickle, with a face aged enough that his beard covered most of his birthmark, freckled enough that the tiny Seckel blended in with the rest of his face, moved to Luke first, offering him an awkward hug. Luke Jr. and Sam stood back nearer the door. Baby Boyd paced around the large octagonal room, looking at his feet mostly. Light shone in from the ward through the windows that lined the room. A silver bar lined the walls as well, and Baby dragged his finger along it, saying, "This is to steady you, right? If you can't walk?"

"Yes, that's right," said the social worker, then added, "I'll leave you all with your father now. If you need anything, the intercom's right here, or go to the nurse's station."

"Thanks," Luke Jr. said, holding the door for her.

Sam started talking to Luke first, telling him he worked now at the Lily mine. This brought a smile to Luke's face. Encouraged, Sam raised his arms in the air to explain how he had to bolt the mine roof, how it sounded when the roof was readying to collapse, how they could see the signs in the face that it might.

Then Sickle talked about the new superstore set to open up in two months, how it might change his job, make him a supervisor. Luke listened, but he didn't say a word. He mostly watched Baby pace. He'd glance out through the observation windows where the nurses and aides moved around the unit, occasionally looking in.

Luke Jr. said, "It's best for you to be in here, Dad. Doctors need to find out what's going on with your kidneys and everything, okay?"

Luke tapped his knees.

Baby said, "I think you'll like it here. It's awful nice."

That's when Luke started to fidget, making signals like he used to.

Sam laughed. "He remembers the signals," he said.

Sickle looked a little cautious but Sam slapped him on the back, and Sickle started laughing, too.

Luke made another signal. Baby yelled out the words, "Trip," "Uppercut," "Take down."

Then Luke made a different signal the boys recognized, too, gripping his left wrist and nodding, holding up two fingers, and they turned to each other. When he made the signal again, this time with more exaggerated movements, pointing those fingers to himself, Baby whispered, "Dad?"

Luke stared at Luke Jr., signaled, but Luke Jr. shook his head.

Luke looked back and forth to Sam and Sickle and gave them the same signal. They shook their heads, too. Luke grabbed Baby's wrist and gave the sign again, again, and each time Baby shook his head, saying "No, no." Luke did it again, violently slapping at his wrist, holding up two fingers, then pointing at himself.

A small group of workers gathered outside the observation windows watching Luke and the boys. Two aides moved their heads close to whisper, one pointing in at Luke. A nurse opened the door, asking, "Everything okay in here?"

Everyone, except Luke, held still. The paging system's hum filled the room along with the buzz of the fluorescent lights, the beeps and whistles of machines in the far-off rooms. Luke looked to the nurse, the boys, tears running down his cheeks.

Sam cleared his throat. Baby said, "My dad wants—"

"Everything's fine," Sickle interrupted. "We got this."

She shut the door.

And Luke gave the signal again, over and over, peering out at the crowd, searching, his eyes like those cocks' eyes just before the tether was loosed.

The Less Said

It was a simple pulley. Not weathered, maybe fixed-eye, with some plastic twine threaded through the sheave. It hung there from a bar, which had been bent in the middle by weight and poor planning. The bar was secured to two trees about five feet apart, wispy-looking quaking aspens with trunks about as big around as an average female's thighs. Smooth like them, too.

Other than that, and the hundreds of empty bullet casings scattered about and piled up in mounds, it looked like any other run-down, ordinary camp. If they were true hunters, they would have recycled their casings instead of wasting them. These guys wouldn't take to sizing and primers. They wouldn't deburr, bell, chamfer. They wouldn't know what a carbide die was. True hunters would have had a proper gambrel hoist for the deer they hung.

They were weekenders. That's if what they hung on that pulley was a whitetail. That's if that's what they crept into the woods to hunt.

2

Two of the dancers from Taylor's Body Shop—one of the only thriving establishments in town—went missing for a whole weekend. Taylor yammered about losing customers. "Get those girls back here. I want them dancing around them poles tonight," he yelled to the other girls and collapsed his scraggy frame into his swivel chair next to the register, licked his thumb, and counted out the stacks of ones and fives again, all of those bills creased deep with sweat and booze. But no one went looking, and the girls returned, a little banged up—scrapes on their knees, bruises circling their ankles—but back to their same routines.

Taylor never asked for the details about where they'd been or coerced them into telling him specifics of who it was that stole them away. He said rumors only made business better for the girls. And him. They'd agreed. "Don't go telling the pigs!" they said, raising their penciled brows to their reflections in the smeared mirrors. Mouths agape, they lined dark the watery edges of their eyes.

Many of the regulars noticed the one girl covered up a little more, was a little tenser when she gave laps.

3

Whitey told everyone Meggie was the best bartender he ever had; she'd tended bar for him the past five years since graduating high school. He called her scrappy. Said she could hold her own.

Meggie heard a group of slick city hunters bragging about some camp they'd landed through a sweet deal. Came in to celebrate. She didn't know where the camp was located. Whitey hadn't heard anything about it. (He missed quite a bit Meggie picked up on.)

"You guys always drink girl's drinks," she chided one evening, as she served these same city hunters their Sloe Screws and Fuzzy Navels. One of the huskier ones ordered tequila just to call her at her game.

"You do the shots with me, though," he said.

"Need some training wheels for that stuff?" She offered him a slice of lemon and slid the salt dip close to his hand. He snatched the shot and gulped it, winced and waved the lemon away. She downed hers and smiled, poured a round for his buddies. "On my tab, ladies," she said. "This is one hundred percent blue." She could tell the other three thought she was just sassy, causing no problems. They told the husky one he needed to lighten up. Whitey nodded.

The guy didn't let it go, though. Stopped in the next afternoon, before the rush. Asked her to come out to the camp for a few drinks after she got off. In the quiet of the dive's dimmed lights, steps from the silent jukebox, and in between the growls of engine breaks on overweight coal trucks creeping their last runs of the day, she politely told him no, put a bottle in his hand. She said, "Drink this on me. No hard feelings?" He stubbed out his cigarette right on the bar, next to the ashtray, and grinned.

The scent of burned wood must have summoned Whitey out from the back. He pushed the guy away, said, "Out," and rubbed the burn with a wet rag.

Meggie knew Whitey loved her. *Like a daughter,* he'd say to people, but she sensed he felt much more. Maybe a little crush. He told her many times not to rile up these kinds of guys during hunting season. He'd said, "They get like bucks in rut, Meggie. You want to keep them happy drunks."

"How bad is it," Meggie said, leaning down to take a closer look at the burn. Whitey mumbled something about matching the stain, something about polyurethane.

Then, finally, he shook his head at her. "What'd I tell you?"

"They're harmless, Whitey. All talk," Meggie said, settling her palm on his worn forearm, feeling his muscles tense up and then slacken under her touch.

4

You take your dog to the wrong party with some assholes from the city who claim you as their new friend, their new hunting buddy, too many thirty packs sucked down, and the next thing you know you're sweating out hops and digging a hole. Next thing you know these new buddies make some sorry excuse for a cross out of some leftover lumber scraps and promise they'll fix it all up real nice. Find a good stone for the marker, too. Maybe even have a service for your dog if you want. Give a little eulogy.

One of them leaves the campsite to find you where you've tried to hide for over an hour at the edge of the Sidle, throwing up your guts, begging your phone to connect to some far-off tower, to have just enough juice to call for help, pleading with your busted ankle to stop its throbbing. He slaps you on the back and says, "Hey, man, I was wasted when I shot him. I'm a prick." You wipe your mouth and start to choke up again on both what you've drunk and what you've swallowed of this crime and you spill it all into the night water, frogs laughing in the dark at how gullible you must have been all your sad life that you'd believe some guys with college degrees and slick cars and six-figure salaries might actually like you for your accent, for how much you know about tracking every single living thing in the woods, for how well you retell old episodes of *Columbo*, your spot-on impression of his squinty eye.

He grabs your hand, shakes it. You can't help lose your shit again and cry like some fox cub caught in a trap, and you let him hug you for a few seconds before you push him away.

Boon was the dog's name. A chocolate Lab. Could look like a bear if you were too sauced up on Yuenglings to see he was just a dog. That was the excuse. That and the fact that the dog wouldn't stop barking the whole time that kid hung there.

"He just wanted to shoot something, Jimmy," one of them admits after you're half-dragged up over the greening slip of the Sidle and back to the fire, to the party. But it was never a party. It was some kind of sport you'd never played. And you'll night terror it for the rest of your life. How you hadn't stopped any of it. How you'd even played along, singing, doing your Peter Falk impressions, figuring out riddles, like it was charades. You'll keep replaying that flash of the gun, the dog's silence, its stillness, and your mind on repeat, screaming inside, "bury Boon before they can do more harm."

"That's how he gets," he continues, poking at the hissing fire, green wood frothing its insides out. "He's got a *screw loose,*" he adds, trying to speak to you in your talk—screw loose, he'd heard you say it about your boss, laughed at it, but what you don't know in that moment is that the real words for what they did, why they did it, will be spoken softly to you months later in an anger management session with the therapist your work sets up for you. She'll say, "This man was a psychopath. What all those men talked you into was some kind of hazing and you shouldn't blame yourself for your part in it. It serves no one to blame yourself like this." She won't know it all because you'll never tell all of it. But this night you go along with *just a screw loose* because in your short twenty-five years you haven't yet grown into the person who has the strength you need to stop any of it. Or maybe you're just shocked into keeping quiet until you need to talk a few months later, give up a name or two to Whitey, the make and model of one of their cars. Maybe you're scared because if you don't go along with their excuses tonight, they'll use you how they've used that kid.

"You've done some pretty sad shit, too," the man next to you says to him.

"I didn't do no weird shit with some local girl," he says and lifts the stick, points it across the fire.

You don't know what they're talking about exactly, but it can't be good considering what you and your dog have just witnessed, what your dog had the sense to bark about.

"She's fine. Back at the bar, serving up drinks again," the man next to you replies. He's husky and slumped, his boots so near to the fire they might catch.

5

"It could be a mandrake," Chick from the Thrift Drug store on the corner of Main and Willow said when Gussy told her about the plant. She squinted, looking closer at the picture of it, and then she whispered, "Was there any semen spilt where you found it?"

Gussy just laughed and shook his finger at her.

She said, "I'm serious."

Gussy said, "I know you are. You and your theories all the time. You sound like Crazy Miss Jean."

"Bring me the whole plant. Root, too," Chick said and winked slowly, dusting off the shelves where the decongestants were lined up.

The guy from Penn State extension told Gussy over the phone, "Mandrakes, if you mean Mandragora, well, they don't grow native here. Bring it in, though, and we'll check out what it is you did find." He'd had them ID mushrooms for him many times when he was first learning to forage—then mostly Armillaria mellea from Galerina marginata—and he trusted what they said. It was growing, though, that mandrake, plain as day, right below where the pulley hung.

Gussy noticed the plant after he saw the pulley, but he didn't tell Chick or the guy from Penn State extension about the pulley or that gambrel he spotted in the high weeds. He didn't tell either of them about the hump of dirt he saw a few yards away, either.

Never can get all that dirt back in the same way after you've buried something.

6

All spring and summer long the campsite sat abandoned. Plenty went there to check it out but all they found besides the hump of dirt, casings, and pulley were some broken, faded lawn chairs and cases of empties, piles of half-burned Styrofoam plates, an old rubber stuck on a limb. Nothing.

7

On the hot and drizzling first day of school, a bus headed to the elementary had to stop hard on the steep grade of the Bee Line Dip to keep from hitting a woman sitting on the middle yellow, half hidden by fog.

The driver toggled open the doors and jumped out, warning the kids to stay put in the hull, to look away. She recognized the young woman in the misty hiss of her headlight scream as one of the dancers from Taylor's Body Shop.

A week or so before, the driver had seen the young woman buying nail polish and hair dye at the store, had somehow gotten into a conversation in line about how much more time the young woman would have to work for Taylor to pay off the one year she'd tried college. She wasn't embarrassed one bit, said it was honest work and that the customers liked French manicures best. She laughed about that. "You'd think they'd like red lips and nails, but nope, they like natural."

It was shocking how much tuition cost. The young woman could've been her. Same eyes. Same bony shoulders she once had. Same small mole at the corner of her eye. She said, "Taylor decided he wants us to dance to seventies songs this week," and shook her head. She was buying neon yellow nail polish, baby blue eye shadow, was planning to dye her hair black. "You can't find white lipstick. Did you ever wear that?" she asked.

The bus driver didn't correct her because, yes, she probably did look about the age of a person who'd been a teenager when pale lipstick and blue eye shadow was the style.

After the young woman paid and grabbed her bags, the bus driver learned from the checkout girl, "She's one of them that was drug out to the woods and kept there for days."

"That right?" the bus driver said and watched the young woman walk through those sliding doors acting like nothing horrid had ever happened to her. The checkout girl explained what she knew. Images flashed up in the bus driver's mind between the scanner beeps and the checkout girl's words and she just kept wanting to say, "Is that true?" but she only nodded and kept grabbing her bags from the merry-go-round as the checkout girl licked her finger and separated new bag after new bag, arranging the items in each empty spot.

The bus driver loaded her groceries into the cart, listening, without crushing the bananas with the family-sized cans of beans, the lettuce with the cantaloupe, the fresh bakery rolls with that rack of bloody ribs.

Later that evening she'd asked her husband, "You know about that? A couple girls from Taylor's kidnapped by some city hunters?"

"They weren't kidnapped," he said, running the washrag over the counter where his coffee had dripped. "They went along with those guys to party. What'd they think was gonna happen?"

It wasn't a question. It was a statement. And it was the last thing he said before she nodded to that place deep in her belly that asked, "You finally gonna leave him?"

She packed up that night, quiet, after he went to sleep.

But sure as shit, the next morning she was scrambling his eggs. How'd he know about those girls? What'd he know? She wanted to ask but didn't. She wanted to throw up in his eggs. She'd heard of cooks spitting in food and never knew how a person could do it. But now maybe she could see how that might happen.

What that checkout girl said had made her stomach ache. And the gooey eggs that morning had made her stomach sicker, so she closed her eyes while they hardened up and didn't look close at them when she plated them with the bacon, the bacon that had suddenly looked so raw and sad.

The young woman had seemed fine at the store. Maybe her hands were shaking a little when she placed that hair dye on the belt, those tiny bottles of nail polish?

She didn't seem fine this morning, though, wiping her eyes, those chipped nails bitten down, neon yellow holding on near at her cuticles.

Her eyes were gone. Nothing there. Drugs of some kind had teased them away, maybe? Or maybe it was what had happened to her at that damn camp?

Her pulse was strong, her breathing shallow.

The bus driver took off her flannel, wrapped it around the young woman's trembling bare shoulders, said, "I got you. Don't you worry. I got you." She yelled back over her shoulder, told the one little girl who'd stepped down out of the bus to get on the radio and call for help. She said, "This young woman needs an ambulance. Tell them that, just say, 'Send an ambulance to the school bus at the Bee Line Dip,' honey. Okay. Would you tell them that?" And the little girl nodded once hard and up those steps she went. She stood by the driver's seat and talked on that mic like she'd done it a thousand times before. She nodded and gave a thumbs-up through those steady windshield wipers to the bus driver. Gave a little smile, too, and the bus driver did everything she could to smile back.

She helped the young woman stand and moved her to the berm, told her to stay put.

She found her flares and told the kids to make her proud and get back, right now, to their assigned seats. "Please, do this for me, okay?"

"Okay," some of them echoed back in unison. Others, wide-eyed, stared ahead.

She eased the bus off the road and pulled the fire blanket from the back of the bus, ran to the young woman and swaddled her up in it. She was shaking all over and crying now, saying, "I'm sorry. I'm sorry."

"Not a goddamned thing to be sorry for," the bus driver said and rocked that young woman like she'd been rocked by her mother when she was a tiny girl.

When the ambulance arrived, thank the Lord one of the EMTs was female because the young woman wasn't going into any closed-up place alone with a man again. No way. No how. She'd shown that when she kicked at the male EMT, who said, "Whoa now," as if the young woman was some damn horse.

The bus driver went home that night and called her brother Whitey to tell him what she'd seen. What she'd heard. Whitey said one word, "Okay." Then he hung up.

He called back ten minutes later, said, "Can you take some time off driving in a few weeks, go down to my place in Florida?"

"Sure," she said. She was due some time off, had collected up comp days for a decade or more. She picked out some shorts and tank tees, two swimsuits that didn't fit, and packed that suitcase she'd unpacked a week or so before, called Steiner's Travel to get a flight south.

8

Delmar's son, Hartley, who always was a little off, found himself lost near the campsite in early fall just as archery season was starting up and asked for help getting back. The men made him sing songs. "Just sing the right one and we'll drive you home," is all he told of the night.

The boy didn't come out of the house for weeks after, and when we asked Delmar how his son was doing, he just shook his head and held a palm up, waving away any more talk of it.

9

No one knew who actually owned the campsite. Hell, it would have been simple to go into the courthouse and ask a few questions, but this was the valley and one never went to the courthouse except to get a marriage license or beagle dog license or do jury duty. More you stir the shit, more it stinks, was what everyone said. So no one was going to ask questions there. Lots of other ways to find out.

10

Cheezer, who volunteered at the library and fixed their computers on the side, found a YouTube page one night after he'd shelved all the returned books and organized the old rental DVDs. He'd stumbled onto the page after laughing through the usual hunting funnies, goofy clips of guys holding beers up to the tongue-lopping mouth of a doe, or a shot of a cigar stuck in the rough muzzle of a slumped bear, or some ass-wipe with a corncob for a dick pissing out through his trousers.

But the ones that he clicked on next shook him up. He watched five clips. Couldn't believe what he saw. A bunch of wasted guys at some campsite messing with people, holding each for hours according to the time stamps on the videos. Saying something about how they'd need to gut them out since they hadn't yet tagged a whitetail. Said hunters couldn't just leave the woods empty-handed, without meat or rack, could they?

Then the men hoisted them up, upside down from each ankle, slow-like. They hung there naked, so long their faces turned colors. A few of them looked like they came close to passing out. All this just to piss on them, or pour beer over them, or spit long lines of chew at them. All this just to make them hang there, begging, ankles wide apart, a permanent marker line drawn from their neck to their pubic bone to show where the cut would've been.

Same thing happened at the end of each clip. They promised they'd let each one go if they'd recite some nursery rhyme, remember some line from a movie, or hum a tune. Some cried, some didn't, but each clip was the same in one way: each person hesitated, unblinking, when they crumpled to the ground and were told they could leave. The men laughed and cheered them on, "Faster, faster, now," watching them take off through the woods when they finally decided they could run.

The next day Cheezer whispered to his other geek friends about how *bad* those movies were. Wouldn't give up the URLs for nothing, though. Said he didn't want no one seeing that.

He also didn't tell them that he recognized one of the girls from Danny Taylor's Body Shop and one from Whitey's bar, even one from his old church youth group. And he recognized a boy, too. A brother of a friend. He also thought he might know where the camp was, based on the gas line clearing in the background.

That evening, he volunteered to lock up and said goodbye to the librarian, watched her unlock her car door, turn on her headlights, drive away. Then he watered the spider plants, careful not to trip on the cascading spiderettes. He shut down the lights over the front stacks and headed back to the blue glow of his laptop to watch the videos a second time just to see if they were really as awful as he'd remembered.

11

When buck season came around again, some local hunters hooked up at Whitey's with this group of smooth-talking city hunters who'd been there the year before.

Whitey had loaded up his favorites on the old jukebox to play for hours. Meggie would always say, "Don't you think they'd like some Lynn Anderson" when Whitey selected classic Hank Williams, Johnny Cash, and especially George Thorogood's crowd-pleasing sing-along, "One Bourbon, One Scotch, One Beer," to gin up the male clientele. She'd belt out the lyrics to Anderson's "(I Never Promised You a) Rose Garden." And Whitey would always laugh, even sing along.

In early October as the leaves burned off their green, showed their true colors, Whitey had talked Meggie into flying south to his trailer in North Florida with his sister, said, "She's fixing up the place. Needs a lady's touch." Meggie had rolled her eyes but she was interested, he could tell. Her family was never one to travel. She'd only been out of the state once for a funeral in Westfield, NY, sadly called Erie Lake's edge her favorite shore. Never been to the beach. He wanted her nowhere near those city hunters until he figured out how to protect her. Didn't want her triggered. She hadn't asked for his protection. She was strong as anyone, but he'd seen how she'd turned jumpy as the weather cooled, as the local archery guys talked of their tracking. Rifle season was coming up quicker than either of them needed. They both knew the city guys would be back, and would be bold. They'd gotten away with a lot the year before. More stories had been coughed up as the summer's shimmer ended. Sickening what went on at that campsite. Sickening.

Meggie had resisted taking his offer at first, said, "November and December are your busiest months. No way I can leave then."

"I'll make do. You trained these two well." He'd pointed to the back where his newest employees were doing inventory.

Meggie had been wonderful with Whitey's brother's kid who'd decided the iron-workers union was not for him, went hippie a little, and had let Whitey know in no uncertain terms that he'd love to take over the bar someday. And Meggie's aunt Carla had been laid off from the mushroom mines and needed quick, good solid work. She was tough, like her niece. She couldn't figure out the new register and she sometimes mixed up orders, but she knew how to handle a rowdy bar crowd. Didn't rattle easily. And if she did, she had, as promised, "a full bitch stare that can shrink nuts."

These local hunters were a group of four that had been called The F.L.O.W. It was simple, the first letters of their last names: Fielding, Lane, O'Tell, and Wise. The name, at first a tease, had stuck, because damn, they had flow in the woods, slow and methodical, silent and still as dots of mercury perched in their stands. And when they put on a drive, they always flushed out the deepest woods game, made money shots sickening-easy for hunters who didn't know their asses from holes in the ground when it came to buck kill strategy.

The F.L.O.W. guys promised the city hunters, "Well, hell yeah, we can get you all to the trophy bucks." They talked for hours about the racks on these beasts, how they'd fed the deer all summer—mineral blocks, apples, shelled corn—and watched them grow.

"You bait them in then," one of the city guys said, laughing.

That almost sealed the deal. O'Tell set his jaw, downed the last of his bourbon, and then quietly corrected the guy. "Baiting is illegal in our county. But I see you don't know that. So allow me to explain." And he went on about the biology of the deer in each season, how they worried about moving herds too far one way or another. Whitey could tell he was pissed. Carla noticed, too, and asked Whitey if he wanted her to shut anyone off or lighten the spike. These local guys despised any talk of baiting during hunting seasons. They were strict with each other about it. "Stop apples in August, stop salt in September" was their mantra. And that meant anything that could be considered bait, from doe urine to spilled maple syrup.

Whitey tried to make light, said, "O'Tell will have you here all night explaining CWD spread."

When the city hunter asked what the hell that was, Fielding made it clear that they'd keep them safe from that fatal wasting disease, said, "We don't want you all getting sick on the game you eat. We're here to help you out best we can."

Convincing.

They told the city hunters they'd show them how to read the rubs the bucks had horned up. Wise said, "It's not anything unnatural that really gets to them, anyway. It's those sugar maples and hemlocks grows them. Yellow birch. They love it."

"They like getting in those oak and hickory stands," Lane added. Eased off his Rolling Rock label, slid it to the wiseass who was pissing off O'Tell.

Whitey loved hearing them talk of their woodsmanship, made him proud to hear how much they *did* know. He'd given up hunting when he could no longer drag his kill out with his own muscle, would not think of hauling it with a towrope by way of a four-wheeler. And even before that, he'd never known how to read the scrapes with any consistency. These guys were exceptional.

"We have old bucks in there that won't show their antlers to no one. But we know where they bed down. We don't take yearlings."

As Wise went on to explain how to age the buck by the shape and contour of the nose, the torso, how it moves through the timbers, the room got warmer, lovely really. He explained Boone and Crockett scaling. The fire in the back hearth—one Whitey'd thought of removing so many times but was ever-talk-ed-into-keeping because Meggie was in love with the crackling of fires he made in it—did exactly what he'd hoped. His nephew stoked the flames, carried in bundle after bundle on his wide trim shoulders, highlights in his long, flowing hair calling up teasing from all the hunters, both local and city, that he'd meet with a flash of his kind, unthreatening smile. It all turned that bar room into a protected cave not at all unlike ones Whitey imagined hunters of long ago sat in, drinking homemade spirits and planning their next day's strategies.

Whitey gave out rounds of drinks for free. The snow came down, guaranteeing prime conditions for tracking whitetails. The windows fogged up with the heat of excited, booze-buzzed breath.

12

Hard to pin down exactly what happened that opening day. Some of the guys got the signals for the drive mixed up, cross-fire, high-powered scopes clouded over, or maybe just buck fever? Somehow those city hunters got shot up by mistake by their own buddies. One, a husky guy, suffered a fatal neck shot. Bled out quick, before ambulances could get to him, so deep into the wood line, so far off the township roads.

The List

*H*illy Luther in crocheted vest and gas-stained jeans, that pale dog walker, mostly high on vanilla extract and spray paint, that callused-foot, trivia-memorizing mind unmarried unmoored human always reciting names of every pet along nine streets on the east side of the river, Hilly Luther in the hazy morning sipping green tea spiked with gin, figuring numbers on a napkin, making a list of the names and sins of all the men wicked and wrong she's bedded with, finally stands up, throws her empty mug into the bin for washing, tips a no-hat-goodbye to the barista, and walks unimpeded by the zigzags of Labradoodles, papillons, and recovery bull terriers, straight to the church with her list. She wants forgiveness for all the things the men did wrong—she wants her priest to grant forgiveness to them publicly at Mass next Sunday.

Father Hayes, in his taut upholstered straight-backed chair with a pencil in one hand and a rosary in the other, stares at the list and nods, moves his lips to name them silently and then closes his eyes. She hasn't uttered her sin if she has one, has just written down those sins of the men listed, and he recognizes each not by their faces but their regular donations: Ronald Banes, fifty each week folded into a football; Mark Simpson, a ten each morning after rosary hour, left near the Virgin and lit candles; Roan Matterhorn's personal checks—his flowing handwriting, enough to pay the electric each week. He can't say the exact words she's written on her list from the pulpit so he's revising them, striking through, erasing, wetting the lead like it will help pull euphemisms from all things religious to form their sins into words he and his congregation can handle.

Hilly taps her finger on the worn wood shelf jamb between them, rattles her knee, and finally grabs the list. Then she pulls the curtain closed on Father Hayes's face and walks out of the blasted confessional. She'll go home and nail the list to her door for the next suitor to read before entering. She whistles the three miles back to her dogs who've shat throughout the house by now, her own dogs, the ones she loves.

Shell

Tiller Shanty peered into the nest, sketching the markings in his journal, erasing, starting again. Spiral. A line bisecting it. There was no mistaking the "M." "M" for his wife's name, Mai. His pencil tip snapped. He struck it with his pen knife to find lead again.

Wind picked up, blowing ribboned cattail leaves sideways, lifting the bill of his hat. He tugged it down, wiped his eyes on the cuff of his shirt, continuing until what he sketched in his journal mirrored what he saw on the eggshell. He trudged out of the marsh, boots deep into the dropped reeds. Two pickups flew by him along the township road, throwing up dust he tried to veil from his eyes. He ached to lift his arm to wave, but he didn't.

When he got home, he slipped into the garage, opened the hickory cabinet that held his notes. He ran a finger along pages of his own corn tassel readings, bark readings, even the tea leaves readings his grandmother's hand had sketched for him when he was small.

There was no crossover. Symbols on red-winged blackbird eggs had their own particular meanings. Still, he searched. He opened the largest notebook, one that held the intricate sketches of his decades reading nests. Mai had decorated it with a male blackbird in flight, had taken hours to get the red and yellow patches exact, the shimmering highlights on the wings. This book held eggshell readings they'd deciphered together, as well as those from Mai's memory of her grandfather's words and notes. Feathers marked pages of symbols for illness, death, but he flipped past those, hoping there was another similar symbol that encoded an altogether different future. Under the bare bulb of the workbench, he scanned every page to find those he'd sketched at the marsh.

After nearly an hour studying the drawings, it became clear. He would lose Mai. How and when would she die? He could not tell.

Mai's calls for their dog, Chạy, seeped in through the cracked window. He shoved the notebooks and sketching journal into the cabinet, leaned against the workbench, his heart hammering this new reality. She appeared in the doorway, listing the garden chores she'd planned for the day—transplanting lungwort and sedum, mulching beds, spraying down the weeds in their stone walks with her vinegar concoction. He took her hands, kissed her.

"Oh," she added, "I forgot to tell you! Happy birthday! What would you like for breakfast?

He couldn't speak. He could only see the markings on that eggshell. He stared into her eyes, hoping that another symbol—one of long life—might call out to him from her deep brown irises.

She said, "Well, I'll surprise you then."

He followed her into the house, trying to ignore the echoing birdcalls jamming their wooded lot, breaking through the battens of their home.

~

Tiller stood at the bedroom window facing the twisting road that led to the cattailed marsh. It was his sixty-third birthday today, a full year since he read that eggshell. This morning's sun dithered behind red and lavender clouds. Down in the yard, Mai wandered through their meticulous beds of perennials. Chạy sniffed every blade, leaf. Mai deadheaded blossoms, staked peonies. Tiller leaned his forehead against the windowpane, closed his eyes.

The screen door below banged. Kibble hit the bowl. Mai murmured something to Chạy. Tiller sat down on the edge of the bed to steady himself. He picked up her robe, holding it to his face, smelling her scent.

Mai's voice broke through. "Are you ever coming down?" Again, he glanced out at the sky.

"On my way," he yelled. It might rain. Storm. Or worse.

In the year since that awful reading, he'd searched the red-winged blackbird eggs in the marsh each morning during the nesting season demanding something might refute what he'd seen, that something might at least hint at how things might unfold, *how* he'd lose her. He studied them for the besom, the sickle, the anchor and waves, claw and chain, more bisected spirals. Would it be a stroke? Heart attack? And when would it happen? His readings had never been wrong, but sometimes he couldn't get the time frame right. Mai was better at that.

Tiller had done everything he could to keep her from harm. Fearing even the yarn store, the library, the meat shop where she ordered pork tenderloin, he drove her everywhere. She didn't mind. "What a handsome chauffeur I have," she'd said one day, poking him in the ribs, laughing. After weeks of it, though, she became annoyed. "It's like you don't trust me to remember my way back?"

"Of course I do."

She chewed at the inside of her cheek, stared out the side window.

"Did you read something on the shells?" she asked.

"No," he said, then placed his hand back on the wheel quickly.

He had to try and be less obvious. She didn't need to know he checked the appliances, the hot water heater, obsessively worried about carbon monoxide poisoning. He had the stairways carpeted, took out the hall tables lest she trip and fall. When she questioned him, he said, "I thought I'd restain these." He snugged up the loose handrails. He stopped parking their vehicles in the garage or anywhere near the house; something in either one might short-circuit and set them aflame in the night. He kept imagining it happening in various ways, her untimely death, the symbols of loss like mottled dots or streaks on a photo's negative he wanted clear, sharp.

The worst time was between the fall and spring clutches when the nests were empty. Still, he walked to the marsh and back each morning, as if an egg would somehow appear.

Nothing—thank goodness—had happened to Mai. No wreck, no accident, no awful diagnosis. But he couldn't shake the thought of her passing ahead of him, leaving him alone. For the past year he'd moved around his life, holding his breath for minutes at a time in a panic until he'd simply found himself lightheaded and exhausted.

~

"You trust your eye," his grandmother had instructed when he was ten. "Trust that tickle in your spine, that shake in your hand when you hover over the signs, see?" She'd held his small hand over the tea leaves, closed her eyes.

Macie Shanty was known in the valley for her gift of "reading the cup," a spaewife. She knew how to read not just coffee grounds and tea leaves but bark, shale, cracks in roads, woodgrains, and corn tassels. She taught Tiller each gift, made him practice with her. He heard many years later from Crazy Miss Jean—one of her students of tasseography—that his grandmother could read eggshells, too, but he'd never watched her do it. When Tiller met Mai, near the end of his tour in Vietnam, they found they had at least one thing in common: divination. Mai and her grandfather had deep sight, too.

"You have eyes for reading," she'd said the first time he'd met her, as she rang up his tab at the bar.

His fellow soldiers laughed. One answered for Tiller, "Yes, he does. And a dick for screwing." Tiller stood there, silent, unable to move or speak while the Filipino band played CCR's "Run Through the Jungle," the harmonica notes yammering through the place.

Mai ignored the other men, shook Tiller's hand. He was sure she couldn't know he was MIBARS, an imagery interpreter. She meant something else. She knew?

The next day, he returned to the bar, asked if she'd like to have dinner, maybe take a walk together. She said, "Of course," and that's when she told him her grandfather had taught her how to read nests.

"I am not so good as he is, but I can teach you. If you like?"

Tiller lifted her hand to his lips and kissed it. He let his breath spill over her knuckles. "I'd be honored," he finally said.

"Oh. Honored," she said, laughing. "Well, we will see."

In the lovely weeks he spent with her, she taught him to read nests—the pair of them poring together over eggshells at a swamp near the base, laughing, making love and promises and plans.

Tiller had to leave without her and it took two years to get Mai to the states, but he predicted, with Mai's help, each step of the bureaucratic craziness with the markings on shells. She read the nests near her, sending sketches of what she saw. He did the same with clutches at the marsh near where he started building their future home. The paperwork came through the day the shells said it would, as did her arrival. The shells also predicted he would quit the military upon returning stateside. It didn't tell him what he'd do next, but he quickly found a job working for the telephone company. Even Mai's first miscarriage, just seven months after they'd settled into their home, was foretold clear and plain on the shell.

That was the first time Tiller kept a reading from her until after the fact.

She had him pull over at the marsh on their way home from the hospital, her empty womb still full-looking. He sat in the truck, waited while she ripped a cattail from a thick stand of them and got back into the cab. She held it across her lap the whole way home and then placed it on their windowsill. "It is the way it has to be. We will keep trying," she said, running a finger along the brown seed head.

By the time the cattail opened, exploding its white fragile insides onto the sill and the floor below, she was pregnant again, as she said she would be.

But the shells showed they'd lose that baby, too. The shells showed three more miscarriages.

Mai was thirty-three with the last pregnancy. The day after he alone saw the broken circle, the bisected spiral to its left, she had made up the crib again. Second trimester.

He could not bear to tell her.

That night bleeding awakened her. He said nothing. She demanded to see the egg.

When they got to the marsh, he held her hand to steady her in the reedy stands of cattails. He shined his flashlight and before he could stop her, she pulled the egg from the nest—something neither ever did—and she threw it against a rock. When Tiller tried to help her from the marsh she simply collapsed, sinking her knees into the brown water. She mumbled something over and over but Tiller couldn't figure out the words, didn't ask her what they meant.

He kept the shell's fragments in his workbench's drawer, fearing if he left them there on the rock, a worse fate would track them.

≂

Every day during nesting season, Tiller and Mai read the eggs of red-winged blackbirds together, and the shells held much good news, too. A job as a language teacher at the branch campus for Mai. Her far-off cousin's move to the States. Tiller's promotion.

Most readings had to do with the growing season, the weather. Some showed their meanings to them immediately. Others took a few days to read, in which case they'd revisit the marsh to see an egg again several times. These eggs, their markings, had predicted the flooded creek banks along the Sidle. They'd predicted the shooting of the albino buck and the massive heart attack the fool who shot it would suffer two months later. Sometimes they'd get hints of names,

places, and other times just images and symbols. A tiny casket. A
boot. A buck. Smashed ditch lilies. A couple held at gunpoint, a
man twisting the neck of a fighting cock, a pregnant woman bleeding. He tried to blink the difficult images away, to rub them from
his eyes, but they stayed. Often, thankfully, there were images of
kindness, of love, of connection: hands touching, a forgiveness, an
embrace, so vague and limited, but filled with joy, and he was lifted
by these.

It got so people would come, even the rich ladies from town,
to try to talk him into making a reading on their destiny. He'd say
he'd let them know if their initials showed up, but it wasn't something he could control. They offered to pay him but he wouldn't take
money for this gift that had been laid upon him.

The marsh sat along a tar-and-chip road about a mile from
their home. Usually, Tiller visited the marsh in the morning to study
the nests alone. Most times he'd take his notebook along and sketch
the egg markings as he viewed them in the low marsh nests. Then
he'd walk back home and make his reading. Sometimes he could
read the eggs quickly, right there, before a blackbird winged him,
swooping down near his head, warning him away.

In the evening, Mai came along, and he'd finalize his reading with her. The wavy lines, the squiggles, and dots on the shells
told of births, deaths, fights, accidents, disasters, needed rain,
healthy crops, windfalls. Sometimes Mai's smile stayed fixed for
the length of their walk back, sometimes her brow remained fur-
rowed. "There are times I wish I didn't know what's to come," she
said one evening. And Tiller told her she didn't have to go along,
that he could read them on his own. And she simply stopped.

He'd also kept a reading from Mai about Mùa hè, the dog they'd lost just after Mai's last miscarriage. Tiller read the sign for cancer, that ugly five-pronged series of lines, the "s" shape next to the sign for a dog—two dots like the stars of Canis Minor. He knew the dog's passing might be days away by the proximity of the signs. At first Tiller thought it might have actually been an "S" for his neighbor down the road, Spencer Singleton, who'd been in his final rounds of chemo, but when Tiller returned home, his beautiful jet-black dog was limp again beside the door. It raised its head briefly as he entered, its tail offering up only two quiet thuds.

Tiller unlaced his boots, wondering if he should tell Mai it would be only days until the dog passed. He stood again watching the dog's labored breathing keeping time with the mantel clock's ticks. He thought he smelled ammonia? Blood?

"She won't drink," Mai said. "She hasn't moved from that spot since you left, Til."

The whole way to the vet's office, Mai whispered into the dog's ear and hummed. The eighty-pound shepherd lay across the bench seat, its head on Mai's lap. Every so often Mai looked out the side window. Tiller could tell she was trying not to break down by the way she closed her eyes, rubbed at her throat.

On the way back home, she kept repeating, "We'll get you fixed up right away, Mùa hè. These pills will help."

Tiller pulled in the drive, shut down the motor. The dog tried to get up but Mai held her to the seat. "Whoa, Mùa hè. Wait."

"It's all through her, Mai."

"I know. But we never know how healing works, right?"

Three days later, the dog could barely lift its head from the floor. Urine leaked from around its back end. That's when Tiller told her about the shell's reading. She nodded, said, "Then we'll go now." And she helped him carry the dog to the truck.

Mùa hè died before they made it to the vet.

In her grief, Mai didn't speak to Tiller for days. When she did, she said, "It was unfair, what you did. Don't ever keep a reading from me again."

"But you said you might rather not know."

"I *want* to know."

She walked out to the garden to tend to her vines.

Years later she could be brought to tears just by the mention of the dog's name. She even mistakenly called Chạy *Mùa hè* several times, her eyes lost in grief. And when Tiller corrected her, she shook her head.

∼

Chạy wagged her tail as she waited at the bottom of the stairs for Tiller to come down. Mai was pouring his coffee when he finally got himself to the kitchen. He sat down, acted like he was scanning the paper. Should he go now? Should he just get it over and done with and see what the eggs showed?

"What were you doing so long up there?"

"Sleeping in."

"Well, happy birthday!" She kissed him on the cheek, set his plate in front of him. "You going to the marsh today for your birthday reading? You missed yesterday."

"No, I went yesterday."

"You did?" she asked. Chạy whined. Mai shushed her.

"Yes."

Mai looked confused, leafing through the mail, sipping her coffee.

Tiller worried again that she had decided to get back to reading nests, that she went to the marsh herself, had seen the same markings. It was true that the last few times he'd returned and tried to show her his sketches, she acted as though she was too busy to help figure out the reading. "You're the expert, Tiller."

"That's not true," he'd said, calling her out, desperate to know if she'd seen something.

"It is."

In fact, one night, after Mai had fallen asleep, he was checking the wiring of the junction box, convincing himself she'd been to the marsh without him, panicking that she'd seen something bad. Earlier that day, he'd been finishing up re-stoning the small footwall along the pond where Mai had misjudged her steps because of her bifocals and fallen in. It had taken longer than he thought to repair, more rock than he'd estimated, and when he drove to the creek bed to harvest more, he came upon Mai on the road to the marsh. She was startled to see him. She said, quickly and stuttering, "I'm looking for mushrooms."

That had been weeks before. Since then, he followed her around the property, always asking where she was going, could he join her?

"I know what I'm doing. You treat me like a child," she'd said.

Now Mai got up from the table, set the letters on the counter. "More coffee?"

"What? No. I'm heading out."

"Are you okay? Have you seen something?" She settled the pot back in its cradle.

"What?"

"Have you seen something that troubles you?"

"No. Nothing much lately."

"No cancer's back for Spencer?" She nudged the dog out of the way, sat back down.

"Mai, Spencer's been in remission for years." He pulled out the crossword page from the paper, slid it over to her.

"But I haven't seen him."

"He was just here the other day. Remember? He brought smoked salmon."

She nodded and grabbed a pencil, tracing the tip of it over the empty spaces on the puzzle. Tiller kissed her cheek and stood. "Well, I guess I'll head out," he said, his words elevated to a question.

She nodded again.

Tiller was exhausted halfway there but forced himself to the entrance just off the road. The wind picked up, sending dust from the berms into his eyes. The first nests he came upon at the more solid end were filled with two eggs each, so he made his way deeper into the thicket, slopping through the marshy mess where cattails swayed as he walked. Larger clutches could always be found within denser cover. An egg jostled loose from one nest near his left knee and he reached for it, watching his hand act on an impulse his heart knew was dead wrong. As he caught it, cupped it there in his palm, he thought, "Put it back, man." But he couldn't. This egg would have to go home with him. He felt its warmth in his hand, knew the spiral was there. He couldn't read it now. He wouldn't. He wrapped it in his handkerchief.

As he walked the long path back, a route farther than the regular road, he did all he could to resist looking at the egg, and when he finally got back home, his T-shirt soaked with sweat, he set it on his workbench.

"Who's there?" Mai yelled out.

"It's me. I'll be there." Tiller quickly closed the door behind him and met Mai in the backyard, where he found her on her knees digging up the flower gardens.

"What are you up to?" Tiller asked.

"I guess I was weeding and—"

"Got a little carried away?"

"I did," Mai said. She smiled, wrinkled her brow. Could she see his worry, his guilt? Was she upset? She'd been asking Tiller to quarter her lilies for weeks, but he was so preoccupied with his safety measures—adding fire extinguishers to each room, checking the outside banisters for rot— he'd put it off.

All at once, Mai started weeping.

"What's wrong, Mai?"

"Nothing."

"I'm sorry, I'll help."

"No. No. Let it go." She got up and ran to the house.

He decided he'd tell her tonight. He'd study the egg first, then he'd show her.

∽

When they first met, Mai had told him how her grandfather predicted many deaths in their village—including his own. In fact, the egg that showed it was one Mai had carried to the states with her.

Back then, she took Tiller to where her village had once been.

He could almost see the scene as she described the day it burned. She'd been afraid to go back for months. She told Tiller she knew it was risky for her to take him there but she had to get something left behind. "Má and Ba, we ran all the way, but when we got here, too late." They saw the skeletal messes, strewn across the weedy growth, in place of what was once, she explained, a gathering of small homes, one of which was her grandfather's, the place she'd lived with him.

"The smell, Tiller. Horrible." She shook her head, squeezed her eyes closed.

He could imagine the scent of charred flesh as she explained more, her voice dropping off with some words, becoming louder with others. She spoke some in her native language, would catch herself, translate into English. At one point she was silent, staring at him. Holding back. What did she see when she looked at him? What wasn't she saying? That American soldiers set that fire?

He said, "I'm sorry," and again, in his best Vietnamese, "*Tôi xin lôi, Mai.*"

With that, she continued describing it. Sparks, flames. Wood burning. Roofs collapsing, screams. "My grandfather, he could not get out fast enough or maybe he was knocked out when the roof collapsed. We don't know. He was found here."

When Tiller heard this, he scratched at that spot on his neck that seemed to always ache when he saw a destroyed village. He never saw these scenes in person, just from the God's-eye view while staring into the lightbox at the post-mission aerial shots.

Mai said, "Wait here." She walked to a tree a few feet beyond the charred leavings and dug at the ground. A small box emerged from the loamy soil, a small tin box he figured held her family's money. He didn't ask what it contained that day as they drove silently back to base. He only heard her tears tap the lid of the box, watched them wash the gray dirt away in lines to reveal a dark green tin.

When Mai finally arrived in the US, he drove her past the marsh, pointing it out in the dark. He carried her over the threshold of the board-and-batten house he'd built while he'd waited for her and straight to their bed. Just after they made love, she rose from the covers, opened her suitcase. She pulled out the now-shiny green tin, and revealed not money, but a journal and a single small blown egg adorned with what he thought at first was some sort of calligraphy, for the markings were much darker than any he'd seen. Then he realized these were the kinds of eggs her grandfather read.

"This is the egg that showed my grandfather's death and the death of our home." Tiller nodded, taking in the markings. "But look here." She turned it over. There he could see what looked like a perfect heart and a "T" and an "M." She grabbed his hand. "This means we were meant for each other. My grandfather said I would someday meet a man named 'T' and fall in love." Certainly, Tiller believed it. He needed to believe the markings on eggs. Back then, knowing even a hint of a certain future centered him.

⌤

This egg on the workbench had nearly the same markings as the one on his birthday a year before. The meaning was clear. He was losing her. He sat staring at it in the light of the garage's overhead buzzing fluorescence. He turned it over and over again. Then, he gingerly wrapped it.

What if he just put the egg back? What if he just started living without the readings?

He didn't want to wake her—Mai had gone upstairs early,

was now surely sleeping. He hadn't heard a sound in hours. He stole out the back of the garage with the egg tucked deep in his coat pocket. He could drive but he didn't want to wake Mai with the sound of the truck starting, so he walked the mile to the marsh, searched for the exact nest with his flashlight beam. When he found it, he placed the egg back in the clutch.

Birds startled and mobbed him, screaming out their annoyance. Instead of taking the time to read another egg, he headed back to the house, walking a longer route, a path through the woods, trying to slow his heartbeat, calm himself, trying to think only of the sound of his footfall on the tar-and-chip road, the bawling of the frogs, a screech owl off to the north, its penetrating song.

In the morning he'd tell Mai about reading the egg a year before and now this one, with the same reading, that had fallen from the nest. Perhaps she'd say they were flawed readings—those of eggs outside the nest—that her grandfather had made the same mistake, misread the egg as telling him to stay in the village the day their village burned. Maybe she'd go back to the marsh in the morning with him. They'd find another egg that would negate the ones he'd seen. Had she ever said that could happen?

He could still see Mai's lips telling the story of her village. He could hear her describe the way her grandfather read eggshells to her, explaining each detail, how he showed her the sign for fire—letting her know that the flame listing left meant actual fire, flame listing right meant passion.

That's when he thought of the candle, and he ran. Mai always lit a candle when she did her nightly reading. Sure, she had always blown it out when she was through, but what if she'd forgotten? His lungs burned like they were set afire. He could barely catch his breath. He already saw in his mind, as he rounded the bend and came upon the entrance of their driveway, the flames sneaking around the baseboards, the smoke billowing from the fractured bedroom windows.

But when he got there, nothing. No smoke, no fire.

From the outside, the house was silent.

Still, he bounded up the steps, the dog following close behind, barking. He flung open the door. When he lunged to her side of the bed, Mai screamed out.

"Mai, Mai, it's me. I thought the house caught fire."

"Who? Who are you?"

"Mai, Mai, it's me," he said, hugging her close despite her hands holding him away.

But she said it again into his neck, barely a whisper, "Who are you?"

He pulled himself away. "Mai?"

She pushed his hands away, but slowly she came to, like she'd been on a drug, or waking from a nightmare. "Tiller?" He realized in that moment he'd seen this in her eyes before. The day he met her on the road. She was lost. She did not remember it was Spencer who dropped off the smoked salmon. And she couldn't remember the ingredients for her favorite banana bread, their phone number, and when he found her wading in the pond, she was confused about how she'd fallen in. All those misplaced things. And earlier today when he saw her in the yard, the perfectly fine plants she'd cultivated and fertilized and watered, uprooted and flung from their beds, their leaves wilting in the sun, their bulbs split, their twisting unearthed rhizomes, like the exposed guts of an animal, surrounding her.

He climbed into bed beside her, fully clothed, smelling of the marsh. She clutched him, her body taut and trembling. Neither of them spoke. Just breathed until their rhythms slowed and met. He didn't know then that for the next seven years he'd hold her many times just like this. Some of those times, she'd recognize him. Other times he'd see she was trying to find her way to him again, and he'd whisper, "It's me, Tiller. I'm here." This would be before he'd move her to the care facility five miles away where he'd set up the blown-out shells on a shelf so she could see them, where he'd read novels to her, where he'd feed her raspberries, and smile and point at the birds on the feeder outside her window.

The Fourth

*H*eat lightning. Mid-summer. Nothing to fear. Storm's not coming. Just the lightning flashing the sky. Aunt Meg, Aunt Mo, and Mom gather up the last of the coconut-frosted cupcakes; the only brownies left are the dried-out ones with nuts. They roll the tops of chip bags, clip them with clothespins from the line, while we chew the juice out of wax-bottle candy and hit shuttlecocks high into the sky. Dad folds lawn chairs and leans them against the porch. The light of his cig makes a string path in the deep dark while fireflies dot around him. He's laughing at Uncle Hank, who's sauced on something more than beer, who's singing, who's talking about heading down to the Eagles to sign the book.

"They open on the holiday?" Aunt Mo asks, singsong voice.

Aunt Meg shakes her head at Uncle Hank. "You've had enough, I'd say."

"What?" he says.

They've probably hit the Echo Spring. Even Uncle Ron looks mellow. I see him smiling a bit by the firelight when Dad calls out, "Hey Uncle Serious, gonna help clean up?" Uncle Ron shakes his head, crosses his ankles, and takes another sip. He smiles and shakes a finger at his Ronnie and Rick sneaking beers from deep in the metal coolers.

Out of nowhere a brilliant Queen Anne's lace lights-up-humungous the sky, then the boom. I watch a line of light zip-wiggle from the treetops to the middle of the big smoky afterburn, blooming again, this time into a blue Allium. Then that boom.

My cousin Keith pretends he's been shot. He falls to the ground. I don't understand at first and then when the next four blooms come together in the sky I'm ready—wait for it—BOOM, BOOM, BOOM, BOOM—and I hold my hand over my heart and fall to the ground. So does my brother and my other cousin, Michelle.

Our moms run to us. They think we've been hit. No, they want us to stop. They keep looking back at Uncle Ron, at Aunt Mo patting his knee, as they pull us along with them to round up my oldest cousins from in the house, Beth and Linda. They hand them the smoke bombs and snakes and we walk together to the alley, under the streetlight. Beth lights one of the small charcoal pills with the end of her cigarette and a snake grows. "He'll be okay," she says of Uncle Ron, but I can't stop turning around to see where our moms have taken him. Is he going to be sick? "No, he just doesn't like those big booms, that's all. He's okay."

The smoke bomb bleeds green fog onto the alley, leaves a green stain on the asphalt. Another bleeds red. Something about the war. "Shell shock," Linda tries to explain but I can't quite, don't quite, know.

Mom says it again, whispers it, "Shell shock," when she's scrubbing out the brownie pan, how hard she's working the edges to get that chocolate from it.

I eat the last of the Jell-O, avoiding the pieces of pears in it. When I lick my finger, I taste the smoke bomb. When she says, "It's these flashbacks he gets," I feel the boom-boom-boom-boom of the fireworks still in my chest. I see Uncle Ron's grimace and my Aunt Mo's arm around his shoulders when we fall fall fall fall to the ground. I see Beth's lit cigarette making those snakes dance, my brother trying to pick up the ash snake without breaking it into so many pieces, into nothing but dust.

Drumming

Dusty Sinclair plunged both of her hands in the steaming liquid, felt the slick softness of the bleached water on her fingers. She wrung the rag, slid it over the counters, nodding, nodding, smiling, nodding, while Elbert chattered on about the men in the green trucks, the wells they were punching into the ground all over the valley, about how he worried their drilling might spoil the Sidle.

"Do you think they'll convince anyone else to sell?" she asked, turning to meet his eyes, knowing he likely wouldn't answer or even look at her. Elbert's eyes met no one's since the incident. He talked. A lot, sometimes. The only way people could tell he took in what *they* said was if they watched him count the syllables of the words as they spoke.

"Marcellus, Utica, what's the difference?" she asked, watching him tap three times for *Marcellus*, three for *Utica*, twice for *difference*. She smiled. "I mean, dif-fer-ence," she repeated. He tapped three times, letting a tiny half smile itch his cheek. Then he pulled out his notebook with his only hand, held it down with his stump, and jotted something.

"One's deep under the other," he said, quiet as pie, and smiled full at his writing.

She stood there in front of him, watched him pull his wallet and change from his pocket. He placed the exact amount on the slip and situated two dollars in the menu holder for her. They'd been in the same study hall their senior year, where he'd often tap out drum solos pretending he was Neil Peart or Phil Collins. She went to see him at the hospital after his stepfather took a Buck knife to the tendons of his wrists for practicing too loud.

The restaurant had just cleared from morning rush. She'd have time to schedule with her doctor. She'd have time to go out back for a smoke. She could hear the dishwasher clanging pans and dishes, water spraying against stainless. She could hear the UPS truck pulling in across the street, the dogs at Herbie's junkyard sounding off their warnings. She could hear the sweet trilling of the kids at the elementary school, outside for gym class.

"Hysterosalpingogram," she said. Elbert's eyes glinted toward hers, and he tapped the counter five times before she slid her hand under his finger. "That's what they want me to have next, Elbert." He tapped gently on the softest part of her palm, once, then again.

She should have been telling her husband this, or her mother, or her best friends.

"Infertile," she said, feeling him tap her skin three times. Her throat stung, but she kept going. She closed her eyes and said, "Empty." He tapped twice.

"I'm so sad," she said. He tapped slowly once, twice, then again. When she opened her eyes, he was staring right into them.

They Didn't Sound Like Themselves for Us

*F*ather Deemer pointed to the paddle on the wall of his office. He'd make an example of us. He was disappointed in us, repeating how we were cream of the crop, honor students, youth group leaders, from hardworking families with parents expecting more from us. But we'd spied on Father Deemer whispering different words as he adjusted his starched clergy collar at faculty meetings. He'd said we were "outliers" and "surprisingly gifted" given from what, where, whom we'd come. Indigents.

We had to look up that word. We weren't indigents. Our parents worked. Some of them two jobs. The day he'd said indigents was the same day we found the meaning of pizzle. We'd been studying *Henry the IV*. Falstaff's lines: "'Sblood, you starveling, you elfskin, you dried neat's tongue, you bull's pizzle, you stockfish! O, for breath to utter what is like thee! You tailor's-yard, you sheath, you bowcase, you vile standing tuck—"

And it was this word, *pizzle*, that dropped us into the office, for we'd said it on the announcements—made it Word of the Day. Swapped out *didapper*. Father Deemer had come up with didapper— he was an avid birder. Students wrote pizzle on the boards, made up songs about pizzles, called each other pizzles until, as the rumor went, the biology teacher, Ms. Lissa Smith-Solomon, walked into Father Deemer's office and said, "You know that means bull penis?" Just a month before, two other girls in the senior class got the wood for making the Word of the Day *gossypol*. The rule was clear: No words related to sex. Gossypol, as we found in our research, was a substance from the cotton plant, but it could be used for birth control.

We knew Father Deemer had had the woodshop teacher drill extra holes into the paddle to make it whistle and sting. The staff never paddled butts but backs of legs. Skin over hamstrings sported welted purple dots that turned yellow in a week. It only took a week.

We leaned into each other, listening to his lecture—"I'd thought better of you"—the sides of our hands touching, our jagged breaths synchronized.

Change of class squeals from mouths and tennis shoe rubber in the hallway, the droning sound of the secretary's secretary voice on the phone.

They were calling in our fathers.

We knew our dads could not be easily reached. They were under the hill, sucking in limestone-dusted coal walls, at the face, bolting the ceiling. They were between union calls, stocking shelves at

Delfry's market, shifting tobacco from cheek to cheek, slicing cardboard boxes open, careful not to puncture the merchandise. They were hauling cement, sniffing the leaking exhaust from a dry-rotted gasket, laughing at friends' voices over the CB, dodging bears who wanted to flag them down, fine their asses for some silly thing like a dim taillight.

"Just give them the wood. I don't have time to come in and talk this over." That's what our dads would surely say, should the secretary somehow get in touch.

They showed, though. One of them couldn't get out from under the hill until second shift came—they were in deep on this cut, the man-trip was slow, and he was a bolter—but he made it.

The "why would you do this" piled up in the corners of their eyes, in their pursed lips, in the way they didn't know what to do with their hands as they listened to Father Deemer explain what we'd done. They shifted on the wooden bench, picked at a piece of dried cement or a nip of tar on their jeans. Their boots seemed too big for their feet, dusty laces weak behind their hooks, ready to give. The skin on their hands callused, cracked, stained with oil or grease or dirt that wouldn't come clean. They nodded in unison, clearing their throats.

"Does it have to be the wood?" one of them said, his voice as far away as the coal tipple, the deep freeze at Delfry's store, the highway's dusty weigh station. They'd all threatened the belt many times, but they'd never laid it upon our skin. "It's just a word." But we all knew, sitting in that office there, how much words, how you said them, mattered.

Father Deemer said, "I suppose detention could be an option as long as this kind of behavior never ever happens again."

"It won't," they said, shaking their heads too far left and right, jumping up from the bench, nearly tripping to his desk, to shake Father Deemer's hand.

Father Deemer raised his, told them, "Sit back down."

They did.

And that's when they apologized for us, made promises, bit at the sides of their cheeks. They spoke in words that stumbled out of their mouths for lack of use, carefully hitting every syllable, no elisions, the "-ing," we always wished they'd use, clear and ringing in our ears.

Sostenuto

There was this section of Dvorak's Symphony No. 9 he could play—a little piano riff from the largo movement he'd kick out when he thought about that woman he knew he shouldn't think about at his real job. He feared there he might hurt. Hurt someone. Hurt something. Might lose his job for being distracted, messing up. But here, at his other job, long after all happy hour Suits left, when the regulars were keeping their heads down, when Cubbie was counting money and glasses and filling coaster holders, and right before last call, he played it. It felt right then. It felt like a Crown Royal rim, licked wet.

They had met in the hallway of this place when he was much younger and she was broken, a waft of warm whiskey. She fell onto him, like sound itself, continued to strike him, for three months like a felt hammer, soft and hard. She was both strings and percussion. He knew he didn't love her. He loved his wife, the woman having daughter after daughter, the woman filled with milk and kindness, open eyes and smile, his soft pedal, his una corda.

But lately, and for some time now, he's considered it may have been the only time he'd really felt love. What he lived before and after her—with his wife and daughters—was commitment. A completely different pedal. Different effect. Different sound altogether. Love with this woman he met in the hallway offered more octaves, hidden extra keys below hinged lids.

Since those nights when this woman taught him about another place where sorrow was sharp, and laughter was insanely regular, and movement between emotions so quick and surprising it left him spent, he had to learn to shift back to his life, his place, his contract with level responsibility. And with this move he'd grown closed and heavy, burdened with life, a home full of girls who became women, wives, mothers, and then, slowly and quickly, left him.

His wife fretted over the dotted harlequin bugs on their cauliflower plants, the hairline faults of their plastered ceiling. So he scraped off the black-and-white eggs, lined up like little keys on the undersides of leaves. He spackled.

But he allowed a small spot for this woman he'd met in the hallway.

It was just that lately the memory of her broke through that place where it was tucked safely in his head. She poured out of him somewhere above his ear. Left a gaping hole there his wife was sure to notice, again. He was becoming reckless with despair, restoring jacks and hammers, capstan screws. These broken pianos reminded him, too often, of her, this unsteady steady woman who made him liquid and tender.

His wife's name drew him in first. Her father, his instructor, mentioned her one day as he practiced Chopin's Prelude, No. 7, A major. Octava was nineteen; he was twenty-one. After their first date—tickets her father could not use to the symphony—they played chopsticks, her fingers stumbling over the keys, the side of her arm barely brushing the side of his. "She'll be your metronome," her father had said, toasting them at their wedding.

Just a few weeks into it with this woman in the hallway, his wife found out. She said she understood, said she'd allow him to leave her if that's what he needed. But he stayed. Left playing piano at that bar every night and took on two jobs, one tuning and repairing uprights and grands, and one cleaning long hallways of the music hall with a mop and rolling bucket of gray water. He made enough money to take good care of his wife, his girls, and still played just one night a month, only for tips. She allowed him this, reluctantly.

And so, once a month he remembers when he fell in love, when he just played piano. And the woman? She sweats his drink, slides beside wispy sheets of music, waves around his head, a sound riding on perpetual sustain. And when he's done, when he's had enough, he walks home, unlocks the door, and finds his way back to his bed, his wife, and lays this open spot of his head on the pillow.

Those Red Boots

*W*hile scouting for prime hunting spots rather than running his regular patrol through town, a sheriff's deputy found the first red boot near the old strip mine's spoil pile. Knew it was Ava Singleton's by the inscription. The sheriff himself called the restaurant where she waitressed. "Don't look good, Reese. They're testing it out for DNA evidence now. Can't get into details over the phone."

Problem was the boot was bloodied. No one knew where Ava was—or the other boot.

Reese Raines believed red boots on the girls would be a big draw. In fact, he had his better half, Arnie, change the logo for the restaurant to feature a wiggling pig's ass end popping out of a shiny red boot. Reese's specialty was pulled pork, but customers had been coming in for close to thirty-five years for an array of dishes: brisket, ribs, sauces that could send your mouth into the deep domain of hot spice bliss. He served the best breakfasts in the whole county. Each egg plate included homemade sausage patties, fresh side. And it was no mystery that people came in to check out the girls serving up this food. He'd been told he had the prettiest, sharpest waitstaff in not just all of Wampum but the whole stretch of the turnpike route.

And. Reese treated his girls like family. Protected them from rude comments when he could. Didn't allow inappropriate touching. Made sure he or one of the male employees walked them to their cars after a late shift so they wouldn't fear the dark side of the lot, the employee section. He complimented them often, out loud, sometimes even in front of customers, on their diligence, their goodwill, always their smarts, and sure, their good looks.

If people didn't know Reese was what Reese's old man would've called an old poof—that he and Arnie Couples were, in fact, a couple—they could likely pin him a pervert for surrounding himself at such an age with girls who could've easily been his granddaughters. He understood that. But the people in Wampum knew better. And the road crewmen who spent paving seasons eating meals there instead of cheaper fast-food chains got to know Reese and his girls really well, dropping such heartening notes in the suggestion boot that said things like, "Reese, you're a hell of a boss to those sweethearts," "Best food and service I ever had," and then, later on, "Damn. Those red boots. Love them, Reese," and "All's perfect here. The food, the price, the girls, clear down to those sweet red boots!"

Arnie had been the one to order the boots in at a special price, had gotten quite a deal from an outfit in Memphis. He owned Books & Boots, a used bookstore and shoe shop not far from Reese's restaurant. Arnie was all about great deals, made the best ones on premium steel-toed work boots for his regular sales with the road workers. He liked to think the books he carried were a source of literary engagement for locals and those drifting. Arnie and Reese worked together. Reese gave out 15-percent-off coupons for Arnie's store. Arnie always made a point to tuck a restaurant flyer into the bags with each sale. Word spread, too, about their businesses. When those red boots for Reese's girls made such a hit, crewmen stopped in at Arnie's asking if they could score a pair for their old ladies back home, wanting, Reese supposed, to take some of what they felt at the restaurant back into their homes with them. But Arnie informed them the boots were exclusive for Reese's waitresses.

Since Arnie had always been so paranoid about people switching up boots and blaming him for a faulty fit, he drew each girl's name in fancy calligraphy on the inside of each boot with a permanent marker. That's how the sheriff's deputy knew: Ava Singleton.

≈

It had all started two days before when Reese got a call from Ava's father. Sunday evening. Slow-go seven o'clock. Bird feeder time. Reese was out filling the suet and thistle feeders, all the hoppers he kept around the restaurant's outdoor patios, dropping seed everywhere, when Gavin, Arnie's nephew who worked delivery for Reese, hollered out, "Got a phone call, Mr. Raines." The kid did that little head-twist neck-crack thing that annoyed the hell out of Reese.

"Well, who the hell is it? I'm busy here with the feeders."

Gavin just stood there, perched on the threshold, letting the damn flies in.

Mr. Singleton's voice was raspy, strained. "Ava hasn't been home since, well, since Friday morning. She didn't get the paper or the mail for two days." He rambled on about how he'd just returned home from his weekend away with his son at a buddy's camp, found the house quiet, empty. Singleton was a well-known worrywart and hoverer and often phoned Reese's private line to check on his daughter. But his tone on this call was straight-out panicked.

Reese interrupted, "Maybe she's staying with a friend. Maybe she's with Darcy or—"

"I've called all her friends. No one knows nothing. She was invited to a party last night. Never showed."

"I'm sure she'll turn up soon enough. Young women are known to change their pretty minds on a dime." He tried to be upbeat, yet sympathetic. He knew all about Ava's mother's long battle with ovarian cancer the year before. Ava had said that her father was barely making it through most days, that he was a basket case. She'd said he wouldn't let her get rid of her mother's clothes. Said he thought she might want to wear them. She'd said, "It's so sad. He can't let her go."

Singleton said, "Can't bear to think something happened to my girl," his voice gurgling like he was drowning in the many awful scenarios.

"You know, maybe she just needed to get away for a few days or something. Clear her head? She had a long weekend, after all. Off tomorrow, too, I think." Reese scrolled through the schedule. Ava had talked up a road trip to the Outer Banks, maybe the whole way down to Hatteras, maybe Ocracoke, right after her mother's funeral. But Reese didn't want to get into that with Singleton. "Yes, I see here she's off tomorrow, too. So maybe she just needed a little vacation, you know? Trip up to Lake Erie or something, right?"

But her father didn't even give time for that thought to settle in. He continued, his voice barely audible, cracking, "She didn't show at church this morning. She was supposed to be a greeter with her aunt like her mother used to do. I, I called the sheriff and re-ported her missing." He could hardly get the words out.

"That's good. Okay. Yes. Good. Anything I can do?"

"I'll let you know, Reese. Thanks." A boy's voice whirred in the background, likely Ava's little brother, and Singleton added, "Oh, yeah, ah, can I use her Employee of the Month photo? Sheriff wants a real recent picture."

"You sure can. You want me to bring it over?" Reese pulled the frame down from the office wall—a smaller version of the one he put up in the dining area. Gavin and Louie, the night cook, had their photos displayed as well. Those three were always in the run-ning each month, always ribbing each other about who would get the big prize for Employee of the Year at the Christmas party Reese threw where he also gave out prizes for all sorts of things like "best smile," "best tips," "best wink," "best team spirit."

The photo was a close-up of the petite brunette with a narrow forehead, angular features. She had a few strands of her long hair dyed a pretty plum shade. Her eyes were dark brown. She was fair as could be. She didn't wear much makeup, but she always covered her lips with a plum color that matched those strands. A pretty little thing.

"I said, you want me to bring it over?" Reese repeated. "Listen, now. I'm sure she's just fine."

"I hope you're right." Singleton shushed his son.

"Now just try to settle down. She'll be back home before you know it."

"I just want her home." The line went dead.

Reese called up Arnie immediately, told him what Mr. Sin-gleton had said.

"Well, do you think she ran away? I mean, who could blame

her?" Arnie asked. Reese heard the sound of running water shut off in the background, the deep inhalation of a cigarette. Arnie couldn't quit those damn Camels. Reese knew he hid them under his sink.

"I have no idea," Reese said, "but I certainly wouldn't blame her if she did. Too much pressure. That father of hers is a mess. His nerves are shot." The sheriff's cruiser rolled into the side lot. "Gotta go. For God's sake. The sheriff just pulled in. And you know she's probably just staying with a friend or something."

"Well, call me back. Let me know what they say."

"Will do."

Upon entering Reese's office, the sheriff walked along the back wall, scanning the framed photos—employees in both silly candid shots and posed ones, the softball team Reese sponsored, a few photos of Reese and Arnie at the yearly New Year's parties. The guy kept patting at his comb-over, adjusting his pants over his paunch.

He cleared his throat, began asking Reese questions about when Ava punched out Friday, if she talked about leaving town. Reese went on and on about how Mr. Singleton could get worked up, citing examples of how he would stop in to see her at break time, sometimes get himself into a crying fit over his dead wife. "Not good for business, that crying, you know?" Reese said.

The sheriff adjusted the walkie-talkie at his shoulder, said, "Well, is there anyone working today who was here on Friday when she left work?"

"Sure. Just a sec." Reese referred to his computer, the state-of-the-art scheduling program Arnie had set up for him. He turned the monitor to face the sheriff, pointing to the highlighted names.

"Oh, great," the sheriff said, squinting to read the screen.

"Three of them are here today," Reese said. "I'll give you numbers for the others."

"Thank you. Can I interview them here?"

"Sure can," Reese said, gathering up his newspapers, folders, stacking them on a corner of his desk, repeating in his head what he'd said to Singleton: It's probably nothing.

~

The office door's window was narrow but if Reese stood a few feet away, a smidgen to the left, he could watch the interviews. Each of his employees appeared unconcerned, as did the sheriff. Afterward, Reese settled into his chair, went over by phone all the possibilities with Arnie. They came to the simple conclusion that Ava had taken off to the shopping outlets. "A big sale on yoga attire." Arnie did that squawk-chuckle, said, "Nervous Nellie Singleton." They weren't about to give it another thought.

But when the state police showed up just after the sheriff's devastating call about that bloodied boot, Reese was a shaking mess. The mood in the room—with the officers' formal, clipped, specific introductions—all dark and sharp and looming.

"Officer Jenks and Officer Snyder," Reese repeated, offering them seats at his large desk. Jenks at least smiled. Snyder didn't.

Reese had to keep sipping his water to wet his dried-out mouth as they went over the timeline. He tried to give detailed answers without rambling, as fear sometimes led him to do. As he waited for Officer Jenks to scribble his notes between questions—he was a lefty who curved his hand nearly upside down as he wrote—he kept imagining blood on the boot, all the ways it might have gotten there.

Snyder, the huskier one, didn't take one note but piped in

with his gravelly voice, catching Reese by surprise. "Okay, so we need to ask a little about her personality, background," he rattled out, dipping his scarred chin a little.

If Snyder had been a customer, Reese may have taken this moment to lighten things up, ask him if he'd maybe split his chin riding a bike as a youngster. Reese had the same kind of scar and he marveled at how his own had grown as he aged, instead of fading away, as some scars do. But Reese just scratched at his own scar, said, "Sure. I know a little of her background, I guess." He flattened out the edges of the blotter on his desk as Jenks flipped through his notes and asked question after question.

"Have you any reason to believe Miss Singleton was involved in drugs?" Jenks asked.

"Of course not," Reese said. The last thing Reese needed was some connection to the awful drug scene that seemed to be venturing closer and closer to Wampum. A new highway, the news had called it, a new drug highway. The man's hand curved tight as he prepared to write more. It looked like it might hurt, crimped up like that. When Jenks looked up at him, he added, "No, I haven't seen any signs of drug dealings around here at the restaurant. Nothing."

Snyder asked, "Was she suicidal in your estimation?"

"No, no, no." Why would they ask *him* that? How could he know that?

"Not depressed or anything?" Jenks added.

She'd shown up for work a few times in the doldrums a month or so back. He understood why after she told him some of what had been going on at home.

"Well, you know, some families get hit hard all at once," Reese said, "and the Singletons are no different." He couldn't get comfortable in the damn chair. "The mother, she died a little while back, and, well, the poor girl has been overwhelmed. She took off a few days here and there since. I hated to lose her presence—she's a customer favorite for sure—so I gave her a lighter schedule. She's bounced back fine. But no, not suicidal, far as I could tell. No, sir."

"Are any of your employees particularly close to Miss Singleton?"

"She gets along with everyone."

"Are there any employees you think might be somehow involved in her disappearance?"

Sweat beaded up on Reese's upper lip. He wanted to wipe it. Of course, they'd need to know his suspicions, but Reese was sure no one he'd hired could possibly steal a girl away.

"I can assure you that no one who works here had anything to do with her disappearance."

"Well, if anyone comes to mind or anything." The officer flipped through his notes again. "For now, we'll need a list of all of your employees and their contact information."

"Sure," Reese said, turning on his computer, running his fingernail through the row of keys to remove what dust might be there. He even blew between the keys, shook his head at his little habits of organization and cleanliness likely only Arnie found endearing. How he wished Arnie was here to calm things. "I mean, you see, I make it a rule to hire only good, decent employees."

"And could you make a list of customers, too, regulars—"

"You mean anyone on the crews?"

"Anybody who comes in and specifically requests to dine at her station or, you know, anyone who might seem suspicious for one reason or another."

"Okay," Reese said, trying to think of anyone fitting that category. Most of Reese's business was male. No one stood out from the rest. The restaurant was situated less than a quarter mile from the interchange, so he always had all sorts of travelers coming in day and night—over-the-roaders, salesmen, crewmen.

"And did she have a locker?"

"Yes, yes," Reese said. He pulled his master key from the desk drawer, jumped up to make his way to the lockers.

"No. You don't need to open it now. We'll get a team in here to go through it for evidence. Don't touch anything, okay?"

Reese's old spotted hands shook. He set the keys on the desk beside the officer's notebook. Shoved his hands in his pockets. "Certainly not. I won't touch a thing."

"If anyone who normally comes in stops coming in, well, let us know that, too, okay?"

"Will do."

"We'll need to stick around and take some further notes, if that's okay with you."

"Why, sure. You can set up right here in my office. You hungry?" Reese asked.

"Not now, but thanks."

～

Customers were in a tizzy, the afternoon crowd abuzz with suspicions, shaking heads, pursing lips, saying "Hell of a thing" as they paid their bills at the register, left additional tips in the red boot Reese kept there for just that reason. As much as he knew he should, Reese couldn't seem to work the room. He spent a good part of the lunch shift in the kitchen throwing spotted utensils back in for a second wash, checking dishes for chips, occasionally heading out to the back patio to update Arnie with a call.

"Do you think it's one of the crew?" Arnie whispered over the phone.

Reese peered in the windows to the booths. One of the regular crew groups sat there eating their regular orders like nothing had happened. "I have no idea. I can't read minds."

"No need to get snippy with me about this. I'm just asking."

Reese interrupted two times when the officers were interviewing the daylight cook—a somewhat arrogant thirty-something guy who'd never once laughed at any joke Reese threw out but had always been punctual—and was relieved to find the men talking calmly, the left-hander still taking notes. No suspicious glances at Reese indicating the cook could be a suspect.

He came in again when they were interviewing one of the waitresses and then when they were questioning Gavin, asking both times if anyone needed more coffee. All shook their heads and continued with what sounded like the same questions they'd asked Reese.

When they seemed to be finished, Reese checked on them again. They both stood in front of the cheat charts.

"What's this?" Snyder asked, pointing at the notes on the two large whiteboards Reese had worked hard to teach the waitresses so that they could increase orders, pump up tips, ensure he'd have lots of returning, happy customers.

"Helps the girls know how to talk to the crewmen, is all."

Snyder dragged a finger down the list of terms. "Eagle shits today? Suggest more expensive dishes?"

"Means it's payday, is all," Reese said, adding a forced shrug of his tired old shoulders that almost kinked his neck. He probably looked like some clown to them, some greedy bastard.

"Okay. That's clever," Snyder said.

All three of them stood there reading over the notes—some Reese had Arnie print out in bold fonts and different colors, some the girls had added in their own messy handwriting.

> Rod-buster (ironworkers): kind, courteous, mostly great tippers, like free refills, risk-takers, climb girders of skyscrapers;
> New-Ops (new operating engineers): particular with everything, especially their silverware, dirty boots, bad tippers, arrogant, but can be won over if you take them seriously.

Seriously was underlined in thick red marker. Reese could feel his face getting hot, his throat thick. He hated how hurtful slang could be and here he was, condoning it, encouraging it, for pity's sake.

> Sticks (carpenters' union guys): particular about temperature, extra ice in drinks, good tippers;
> Tube Dogs (tunnel workers): order the same thing every time, no salads, steal extra creamers.

Snyder pointed to the little bubble additions the girls wrote: *"kitty cat"=woman on the jobsite, "dime piece"=good-looking girl, a "ten."* Jenks opened his tablet, made a note. Reese tried to see what he was scratching there.

Snyder's rattling made Reese flinch. "Any of these men seem to show her more attention than others?"

"Not that I've noticed, no."

"We have to head out now, but you'll be seeing a tech later who'll go over her locker, okay?" Jenks said.

"Of course, whatever you have to do."

After the investigating officers left, Reese called a quick meeting in the kitchen, reminding everyone to keep an ear and eye out for the strange, the iffy, shifty, and suspicious.

But that only made things worse. Louie stared at everyone who came through the door, not keeping track of his own feet, and once tripped, sending a basinful of dirty dishes all over the floor. Gavin's cracking of his neck and his knuckles got worse. The girls were jumpy. They started copying entire orders, taking note of the kinds of jeans the men wore, types of sunglasses, spending their whole breaks transcribing the words they heard.

And this amped up the customers' paranoia as well. They talked about where they'd last seen this one or that one from the crew, how dark this one's eyes were, how piercing blue that one's were, how two of them had rough beards the whole way down their necks, or how some of them loaded uppercuts rather than side pouches when they chewed their snuff, as if any of these things could point to the kind of evil it took to kidnap a girl and do something awful to her. After all, as time passed, that's what everyone believed happened.

She didn't go off on her own. She was taken.

One of the UPS guys swore he saw part of a restaurant uniform along the turnpike route, was sure he spotted "those little fringe balls." Reese's stomach flipped.

Reese had gotten a hell of a deal on the old cheering outfits at an auction when the two local high schools merged, went from being the Red and Black Wildcats and Purple and Gold Sabers to the

Black and Gold Eagles. The uniforms were a little ragged from wear but the girls loved prettying up and squeezing into them. Some had even worn them just a few years before as Wildcats; others had never been cheerleaders and now was their chance. He had Sally Price at the Seams New shop reline them, cut the tops shorter to show a little midriff, add some fringe balls to the hems of the miniskirts—made them look kind of retro but brand new, too.

The UPS guy came back in and delivered what it really was he'd seen. Just part of an old blanket. He pulled the wet, cinder-covered thing out of a paper grocery bag and said, "I'll keep looking." Reese called Arnie and told him and Arnie said, "I'm just sick over this."

"Me too, Arnie. Me, too."

~

Two days later, one of the girls, Aimee, the closest to Ava, met Reese in his office, took hold of his forearms with her tiny hands, fingernails painted same red as her boots, clutched his skin so hard he thought sure he'd bruise, asked, "You sure? You sure it isn't one of them on the crew, Mr. Raines?"

"Hell no, sweetie. I'd know it if someone capable of harming one of you girls was within my range."

"Okay," she said, nodding, smoothing down the front of her skirt. "Okay."

He wanted to hug her but he didn't. He just said, "Now get out there and don't worry." She ran her fingertips across the ball fringe.

"Okay, Mr. Raines. Will do!"

He added, before she got through the door, "These are good solid men. Just like anyone else trying to do their work and get back home to their kids and wives again."

She gave him a thumbs-up.

The problem was Reese made a good part of his business from traveling workmen. He didn't want to do anything to push away these mining crews, ironworkers, and members of the carpenters' union.

But it was the first time he'd ever seen Wampum truly turn on a group. Even decades before, during the AIDS scare, in those rough years when people across the nation steered clear of any business owned by homosexuals, Arnie and Reese were supported by the people of Wampum, and because they were highly recommended by the locals, the visitors patronized them, too.

When Ava went missing, though, Reese's voicemail filled up, both at home and at the restaurant. Cards poured in. Customers stopped by the restaurant and at Reese's home to assure him they were praying for Ava's safe return and strength for Reese, too, for all the worry he must be feeling. But they were very clear on what they felt Reese should do, and pronto. Close down the business to these guys. Put up a sign. Do what's right and proper.

The crewmen didn't help themselves. At the bars, some made jokes about how they'd like to steal a few of "those red boot girls" and take them to their next post. One said a girl Ava's size could be easily hidden underneath the concrete and no one would ever know. "That'd be a lean mix." Stupid bar talk, he was likely kidding, but it made everyone worry. Other businesses wouldn't serve them, wouldn't allow them to congregate in groups, so they were permanently kicked out of a few places. Two were even turned away at the Presbyterian Church service.

Reese only had trouble with one man, not a trucker or a crewman, but some freeloader who refused to pay his bill. He said one of the girls was "dumb as a doornail," swore she'd shortchanged him. Reese found out he'd also made a disgusting proposition to this waitress when she went out to the lot for her smoke break.

"He's still out there," Aimee said. Gavin and Louie both offered to scare the guy off, but Reese said, "I'll take care of this." He was searing mad when he got closer to the truck, heard the music blaring from the cab, and he walked straight to it, his hand on the buckle-snap of his .357 holster to let the asshole know he meant business. He gave him a talking-to and came back in while the girls watched from the windows.

He called 911 with the guy's first name and license plate number. A few hours later, the sheriff's deputy stopped by. "Not our guy. He was in upstate New York when she was last seen here in Wampum. Keep a lookout, though."

The deputy made his trip count, ordered two BBQ sandwiches to go, dropped a few bucks in the red boot, and refolded his bag, tighter. "We all have to be paying attention to every little thing right now."

"Exactly," Reese said. "I'm on it."

Ava's father called the restaurant every evening, updating Reese on how many culverts they'd checked, how they'd rescanned the creek beds, how the divers at the cove found nothing despite all the anonymous tips. He said he might drive up north to visit his old neighbor, some psychic or fortune teller named Tiller Shanty, who lived near some magical creek and could read the shells of red-winged blackbird eggs to find the missing. It was tough to hear the agonizing hopefulness in his voice.

Reese would stare at Ava's eleven-by-fourteen framed Employee of the Month photo as he listened to Singleton go on and on. Reese had waffled on whether to take the framed photo down from the front room or not and decided, in the end, to take it to the back, along with Louie's and Gavin's. No one needed to be reminded that she was gone. Same photo was used for the flyers posted all over town.

Reese always ended each call with, "Don't you worry. I'll keep a lookout. For anything."

"I know you will," Ava's father said, and then quickly added, on nearly every call, "So you still think it's safe for the other girls to be around those men 'til we find out more?"

"I can assure you if one of these workers took your girl, I'd know it."

"Thanks so much, Reese. I know you're invested here. I know you'll do the right thing."

~

Weeks later, when they finally got around to mowing berms, the township guys found the other red boot in a ditch line four miles from the first. It had gotten caught in the brush mower—part of it ripped to smithereens. There was a note tucked deep in the toe. The law didn't want to release to the public what was scribbled on it, but when they called Reese in for questioning, this time to the barracks, they showed him the note, hoping he could throw some light on it.

It read, "I just go crazy when I see you in those boots." Reese's legs quivered when he read that. His mind flinched.

God, how different that pretty red boot looked clawed up into pieces on the evidence table than on Reese's girls' feet, polished, clomping from one table to the next.

"Did you see anyone giving Miss Singleton a note?" Jenks

asked, scribbling with that left hand again while another man, whose name Reese didn't catch, stood quietly at the door in his suit and striped tie, his white shirt collar nicely pressed.

"No," Reese said. And he hadn't. But he did know plenty of customers found some merriment in slipping a five or ten into a girl's boot as their tip. And that paper was from the notepads used at the restaurant for the suggestion boot. That he could tell them. That he knew.

"Have you noted anyone obsessed with the red boots?" Jenks asked, looking at his papers, not Reese.

What could Reese say? No one could keep their eyes off the girls in those boots when they performed their choreographed dances for birthdays, retirements, promotions, and high tippers. "No one in particular," Reese said.

"Keep an eye on things, okay? Maybe someone says something, does something suspicious, and you'll let us know right away?" Jenks said, placing his pen on the desk, reaching to shake Reese's sweaty hand.

"Absolutely." For pity's sake, that's all he'd been doing every minute of the day.

"And we'll need handwriting samples from each of the employees," Jenks said, leading Reese out the door. "But don't tell them we found a note. Don't mention that to anyone until we've completed our work, okay?"

"Sure. Whatever you need."

～

Reese and Arnie stood at the office door and watched as each employee wrote out a fake order including all the letters in that note.

"What are they looking for, do you suppose?" Arnie asked, straightening his narrow shoulders, pushing his black-rimmed glasses up the bridge of his nose. His pale green irises always seemed larger than normal through those thick lenses, just as his nose always seemed larger than normal until he took the glasses off for bed. How Reese just wanted the day to be over. How he wanted no secrets between them. To be munching on caramel corn, to be stretched out on his side of the bed, annoying Arnie with the crumbs, and laughing at their box set of old *Soap* episodes. But the day wouldn't be done for hours and instead of ending up at Arnie's, as he sometimes did, Reese would go to his own house.

Never moving in together seemed so silly right now.

"I'm not sure," Reese answered, trying hard to keep from holding his breath in that way Arnie noticed all the time. He stuck his hands in his pockets, too, to keep Arnie from seeing them shake.

Earlier that day, he'd given the news crews as much information as he could, making sure to focus on all of the safety measures he had in place for the girls, but they were hell-bent on connecting Ava's story to the rape two years before of the waitress at Taylor's strip joint thirty-five miles away near Brinie Furnace. The perp ended up being her boyfriend and the case was closed, but they brought it up anyway.

On the evening news, "Local waitress still missing" ticked across the bottom of the screen in bold letters, as well as a banner reading "Second Boot Found," while some B-roll of Reese's awning, zoomed into the red boots, filled the screen. The reporter offered a few details. The sheriff gave a short statement. They cut to customers babbling: "It was only a matter of time until something like this happened." More B-roll of his other waitresses walking out the door after their shift with those boots on, zooming in on their back ends, a voice-over of the reporter explaining where the boots had been found. They cut to an old clip of Taylor's Body Shop. It was only then that they added Reese saying—completely out of context—"She was a customer favorite!" followed by a still of her Employee of the Month photo.

"Who you suppose took her?" Arnie asked as they sat, side by side, in front of the TV set in the office.

"They didn't use half of what I said. I do everything I can to keep those girls safe, and look, look how they're making it seem."

Arnie grabbed the remote, flicked off the TV. "Let's get back to work." He stood on his tiptoes and kissed Reese on the forehead, the end of his nose. When he smiled, Reese tried to smile back. But he couldn't seem to. Arnie grabbed Reese's hands and gave them a good squeeze. Reese placed his worn-out forehead on Arnie's shoulder and they stood that way for several minutes, Arnie's warm hand on his neck, until Reese cleared his throat and stood up straight again.

"You're right," Reese said. "Nothing more we can do about this right now."

～

The handwriting samples showed nothing. So Reese studied everyone even more closely, listening to each word, looking into everyone's eyes. But it took its toll on him. Nighttime was the worst. Reese couldn't seem to get his mind to slow down. He'd jump up, three in the morning, make a note about a man who seemed a little off when he paid his bill, another who had tiny cuts on his hands that looked worrisome. Without thinking of the hour, he called Arnie one night, said, "Just can't still my head." He rambled on about a group of bikers he'd served nearly a year before, trying to remember where they were from, what was written on their leather vests, and Arnie remembered the guys—The Brigade—said they'd bought some books on the history of bridges, seemed harmless.

After a full week of sleepless nights, dallying in the worry of who took Ava and trying to puzzle it out alone, Reese asked Arnie to stay over. He and Arnie had decided early on to keep their own homes. Arnie had pushed back once when he had a few too many drinks, saying it was ridiculous to worry about how the dead would feel about what was going on in their family home, saying, "Everyone knows what we are, Reese. Having separate houses isn't serving anything." But that next morning, in a soberer state, Arnie had called, said, "Hey you, just forget about my complaining last night. We are as different with ideas about keeping house as any two could be. I'm fine if it's what you want."

Now Arnie said yes to Reese's request, and it was so nice to have him right there in bed to talk to when he woke with a chest-thumping dream. He'd touch Arnie's shoulder and Arnie would wake instantly, click on the lamp, grab his glasses. Then he'd turn to Reese, lean up on one skinny elbow, and say, "Now, come on, what's troubling you?"

They'd talk it through. Arnie would lay a hand on Reese's heart and will it to slow down, or he'd snuggle in against Reese's side, warm as can be, and say, "Go to sleep now. We'll go over this tomorrow with our coffee, okay?"

After a string of nights, though, Arnie's eyes were bloodshot. He yawned the whole way through breakfast. Reese said, "You don't need to stay here and babysit me. One of us should be getting some sleep."

One morning, just after the brunch rush, Gavin was loading up the delivery van when Reese caught a glimpse of him talking to one of the girls on her smoke break. It was the way the kid stared at her when she puffed Os with her smoke, the way he watched her tuck the pack of cigs back in her boot.

Reese raced to the back office, poured himself a cup of coffee, nearly spilling it for all the shaking, and sat down at the computer to weed through weeks of timesheets and Gavin's delivery schedule. Ava had been scheduled to work until 11:00 p.m. the night she went missing. Reese already knew that. What he didn't know was where Gavin delivered the next day or if he'd even come into work. He grabbed the order folder, scanned it, trying to push down that instant festering in his gut and that awful, awful "could be" that clogged the back of his throat.

Butler. That's where Gavin was the next day. And Cranberry. That told Reese nothing. But then he saw the note of complaint, dated the same day, from one of the businesses. Mixed-up delivery orders. He'd talked with Gavin about just that.

A good part of Reese's business went into the city for corporate shindigs where the big-time operators wanted to appear down-to-earth, and pulled pork was a great menu selection for that kind of spin. Gavin made a delivery into the city three times a week, sometimes five, but it was nothing to send him the whole way up to Oil City. Arnie's sister warned Gavin might get lost easily, but Arnie promised, "Don't worry. The kid's solid. It's just that she's so overprotective she's nearly ruined him. I told her to let him sign up for one of the over-the-road crews. She said he needs a safe environment to work in, being like he is." He was shy and peculiar, had these terrible headaches that put him out of commission for days, and of course he had that obsessive knuckle and neck cracking and that way of repeating everything—but he worked out great from the start. Reese always gave him good directions since the GPS wasn't always clear, strict instructions for deliveries, a script of sorts. He even had him memorize lines. He kept him busy. He heard back from every customer that Gavin was prompt, polite, and helpful. In fact, they raved about him.

Reese had called Gavin in to talk about the delivery mix-ups. Right there on the note of complaint, Reese's handwriting read, "Reprimanded."

"Now, listen," he'd said, "I can't have this kind of mistake happen again, okay?"

"I know. I'm really so, so sorry." Gavin started crying, covering his face with his hands, a reaction Reese had thought strange at the time.

Reese had comforted him. He remembered thinking the poor kid would call off another three days for some headache. It had happened before when he'd misted bleach all over a stack of black aprons. Arnie and his sister were convinced the headaches came on with stress. But Gavin hadn't gotten a headache after that reprimand and he hadn't messed up another order.

But the more Reese thought about it, he had to admit Gavin loved seeing those girls in the red boots and unlike Reese's other male employees, he stared a little longer at them from his order post while he took down directions from phone-in customers. Reese had even kidded him about it early on when the boots were brand new.

"They draw you in, yessir," Reese had said.

"They sure do," Gavin replied, cracking his neck. "Sure do. Sure do."

And now Reese remembered how once, the girls pulled Gavin

into their routine. His face flamed red. Customers cheered. One of the girls ended the performance by giving him a peck on the cheek. He shook his head like he did and walked away grinning.

Reese took the master key for the lockers from his office drawer—the one he'd given to the tech that had checked Ava's locker weeks before—and went straight to Gavin's. At first he was picking at things, trying to keep it all intact, then he started rummaging through. He found only brochures for upcoming vintage truck shows, a few notes for prices on exhausts and chrome bumpers, a card from an autobody outfit that did custom paint jobs, and several photos of Gavin's old '79 F-100 he'd been overhauling.

Of course, Reese shouldn't be doing this. He was told specifically by the law what to do if he found something suspicious or had some new idea about the case. Gavin wouldn't be back for at least two hours. Reese grabbed the keys to the truck just hanging there on the locker hook and headed out to the jacked-up two-tone green-on-green Ford in the back lot. He nearly fell getting up into the thing. Gavin had it lifted well over legal limit. Sitting there in the cab on that pristine reupholstered bench seat, he shook uncontrollably again, sweating, holding his breath, remembering to breathe. He leaned over and checked the glove box first. A little flashlight. Owner's card and registration in old dusty plastic. A few napkins. He felt under the seat, behind it, under the visors, everywhere.

The truck was clean, no sign of Ava Singleton having been in there.

As Reese came back into the restaurant by the backdoor entrance, Aimee, the little wisp of a thing, shouted, "What's up, Mr. Raines? Geez, sorry, did I scare you?"

"No, of course not," Reese said. But he couldn't help turning away when he saw her slide on those boots. "You work 'til eleven tonight?"

"Yep."

"Well, now, you have a good shift." He took a deep breath, forced a smile. "You look different somehow. Did you get your hair done different?"

"I sure did."

"Well, I like it." He needed her to leave.

"Aw. Thanks, Mr. Raines," she said and sashayed out of the room, boots clicking.

Reese's legs were rubber. He sat down at the desk to catch his breath.

Then, when he could move without falling over, he got up and put the keys back in Gavin's locker, tried to get it looking like it had—taping those pictures of the truck back up like he'd had them.

That's when Reese found the newspaper clipping with a photo of Gavin and Ava in the very back of the locker. It was from a fundraiser they'd held at the restaurant nearly a year before. Reese had said to the photographer, "We gotta get those red boots in the picture. Gavin, pick her up."

"Me?" Gavin had said.

Reese encouraged him. "Go ahead."

There was Gavin, cradling Ava in his lanky arms. His hair, cropped short to the sides and long and wavy on top, was not much different from the way Reese wore his when he was his age. Ava gave a thumbs-up, big smile on her face. Gavin wasn't looking at the camera, though, or at Ava's face. His head was turned slightly in the direction of those boots she wore.

Reese sat down at his desk, his heart thudding like it was about to explode wide open. Why did he insist on having those red boots in the picture? Why did he tell Gavin to pick her up?

Reese folded the news clip, pushed it into his pocket. He picked up the phone, started dialing the number on the card that the investigator had given him after the first interview. He leaned the card on the photo of him and Arnie taken on vacation at Lake Erie three summers before, a hungry crowd of seagulls hovering around them. When the machine answered, Reese panicked and hung up. Then he dialed Arnie's number.

"We have to talk," Reese said.

"What's wrong? You sound upset."

"I can't talk about it on the phone or here at work."

"Okay, come over to the store," Arnie said. "I'll get one of the girls to cover the register."

Reese hung up without telling him goodbye.

~

When he and Arnie got to the back room, among all those boxes and boxes of boots on shelf after shelf, all those dusty books wanting to find another lap to settle into, Reese pulled out the clipping, unfolding it with his trembling hands, and said, "Listen, about the boots—"

"Did they find her?"

"No. Not yet. But I think I have an idea of what might have happened."

"My God, what? Tell me."

Reese held the clipping in his hands and began, "The girls, you know, they're all beautiful girls. And all the men at the restaurant, well, hell, they can't keep their eyes off of them. The way they look in those uniforms, those fine red boots, I mean, and the way they doll themselves up for customers, and I know Gavin sees that—I mean, I've seen how he is around them."

Arnie folded his arms and squinted. Why did he have to squint like that?

"I mean, Arnie, you know. Well, you wouldn't know, I guess, but I've noticed how he looks at them, you know, and they, well, he's a typical young man, right, and so, he's, of course, he's mightily attracted to them, too."

Arnie rolled his lips in, then looked bemused somehow, as if Reese was joking.

Reese continued. "I think, maybe, the girls feel a little sorry for him, and they sometimes pay him too much attention. More than he should get, maybe. You know? Especially, now that I think back, especially Ava, and I think it makes him a little crazy, you know, having them all around him all the time, teasing him about this and that"—Arnie's mouth opened slightly as if a word or two might be tripped up there—"and, well, on the day Ava didn't show for work, Gavin messed up orders and was not acting like himself and—"

Arnie held up his palms to Reese, said, "Do you hear yourself?" He snugged his tie. "My God. What are you saying? Remember, this boy is not your family, but he's mine." He stepped back from Reese, placed his hands on his desk. Was he going to pass out?

Reese flattened the clipping on Arnie's desk next to Arnie's hands. "I'm saying it could be him. Listen, there was this note in that second boot they found."

"What? I didn't hear about a note." Arnie picked up the clipping and set it back down.

"I wasn't allowed to tell anyone about it."

"What did it say? My God. That's why they asked for handwriting samples? Was it Gavin's handwriting?"

"I don't know," Reese said.

"Well, what did it say?"

"It said, ah, something like, I just go crazy when I see you in those boots."

"Well, that could be any number of your regulars," Arnie said. "It could be anyone."

"I know. I'm just saying, I think we need to consider—"

"They checked Gavin out, didn't they? Didn't they question him? I thought all of your people were cleared. I thought you said everyone's handwriting cleared?"

"I thought they did."

Arnie took off his glasses, fiddled with the frames. He moved to the stacks and straightened up the boxes. "Do what you have to do. Go to the cops."

"I don't want to go to the cops yet." Reese reached out to grab Arnie's elbow, but Arnie kept moving the books around. "I thought maybe you could talk to Gavin first. Find out, you know, where he saw her last."

"*You* talk to him," Arnie said. "You think he did this. You do it." Arnie ran his fingers through his hair. He dropped his arms at his sides, started pulling at his shirt cuffs. "My God. Really, this is, this is. But, hey, if you think you have, do you have, anything on Gavin? I mean, what? Has he told you something?"

Reese reached out again, but Arnie put up a hand to stop him.

"I just thought maybe we could talk to him tonight," Reese said.

Arnie stood there pulling at some thread on his cuff. Finally, he jerked up his chin, closed his eyes, said, "I, I—let me think about this. My God." He moved to his desk, scanned his schedule. "I have a meeting I can't cancel with that outfit, that acupuncturist and massage group?" He tapped his finger on the date book. "Okay? And then after that I'll have Gavin over to talk and you, you can ask him whatever you want, but I know he didn't do anything to Ava. He's a good young man."

"I know."

But Reese knew Arnie was wondering, too.

Arnie handed Reese the clipping. Reese leaned in and kissed his forehead just as light as he could. Then he left him there in those stacks.

～

That evening, Arnie had Reese and Gavin over for a late supper and beers at his tiny apartment. He went to the trouble of making pork chops and fried potatoes and the whole space smelled like angry thick grease. Arnie knocked over the can of green beans trying to get the lid cut off. Gavin jumped in and cleaned up the mess. Arnie stared at Reese over the kid's head.

They talked a little of the work Gavin was doing on the truck. They talked about the rain, how it hadn't let up for days.

Just as Reese's stomach was starting to settle enough to consider eating, Arnie shot him a look. He clearly wanted him to start with the questions.

Reese moved his beer a little to the left, the right. "So, you and Ava Singleton were close, weren't ya?"

Gavin cracked his knuckles, then said, "Yeah, I guess I thought we were close. Did you think she liked me?"

Reese peppered his potatoes, settled the shaker back in its slot, said, "Yeah, yeah, sure I did. I think she liked you a lot. I told your Uncle Arnie as much." Reese had never mentioned anything of the sort to Arnie.

Reese asked, "What do you think happened to her?"

Gavin shifted in his chair, adjusted his napkin on his lap. "Well, I don't know. I mean, hey, maybe she ran away, huh?" He took a sip of his beer. "She always said she wanted to go see those big sequoias. Or maybe live in those Outer Banks, in some beach house." He tried to smile. "Maybe?"

Reese had to get out of the room when Gavin paused, when he saw the way his eyes flicked like that as he said "Maybe," as if searching to see if Reese would believe it. Arnie took off his glasses, rubbed his eyes, put his glasses back on.

"So I didn't know so much could be known about a person from how they cross their Ts," Arnie said, carefully buttering his roll.

Reese glanced at Gavin, but Gavin just cut his pork chop.

"I mean," Arnie continued, "I wonder what it would be like to be a person who's paid to do that sort of work—analyzing handwriting."

Gavin wiped his mouth. Took another sip.

Arnie pulled his roll apart. Reese had no idea where he was heading next so he just stayed quiet, pulled his own roll apart.

Arnie asked, "So what did those policemen have you write up?"

"What?"

"You know, when the police had you all write something up for a handwriting sample. What was it?"

"I didn't do no sample," Gavin said. "They must've done it while I was on delivery, maybe."

Arnie placed his palms on the table. He spit out, "Reese thinks maybe you were the last to see Ava alive. Were ya?"

Gavin moved a chunk of meat around in the ketchup on his plate. Then, out of nowhere, he started weeping.

"Hey, hey, hey," Arnie said, then shot a look Reese couldn't quite read.

"She said she liked me plenty of times, Uncle Arnie."

Reese looked down at his plate. He couldn't bear to see the kid's face. Or Arnie's.

"Okay, but what happened that night?" Arnie's voice was steady, calm.

"So I saw her walking home after she and Louie locked up and asked her if she wanted a ride the rest of the way. She never took me up on it before." He shook his head and Reese stayed perfectly still, hoping the kid would keep talking. The refrigerator started up that awful rattle, its old dying compressor, Reese figured. Arnie was staring at Reese now, sweat gathering on his forehead.

"We stopped out at the ramps, you know," Gavin said. "Remember, Mr. Raines?" He looked straight at Reese then, the rims of his eyes reddened. "Remember how she always said the highway sounded like the ocean? How she said you could hear it best at the ramps. How we teased her about that?"

Reese did remember. After she told them that, he himself had taken a walk on the route she walked home. When he got just under the overpass, Reese had closed his eyes, listened. She was right. The traffic sounded just like the surf.

Reese gave a quick nod.

"Did she want to stop there?" Arnie asked. "At the ramps?"

"She didn't say she didn't."

"Okay," Arnie answered, arranging his utensils over the sides of his plate.

"So, we were just talking about the truck, and she kept saying"—he stopped, hitching now—"she kept saying how high it was off the ground, and I told her how long I'd saved up for those wheels and tires and—"

"And what?" Arnie asked.

"And I asked her if she read the note I'd put in her boot."

"You put a note in her boot?" Reese asked.

"Yeah, and she tugged her boot off real quick to see if I did, and then she found it." He stopped and swallowed hard. "She read it and she laughed." He looked to Reese and smiled a little. "Then she leaned over and kissed me on the cheek."

He stopped, put his hand to his glass but didn't lift it to drink.

"Then she stuck that note back in her boot and tugged it on again and I thought she wanted to, you know, *do* something, and so I put my hand on hers and she held mine and we talked about, I don't know, all sorts of things, her mom's cancer, her dog she'd just put down. You know, her old Lab she kept pictures of on her locker?"

Gavin nodded at both of them. His head like some bobble toy. Reese's knees buzzed.

"And she was real sad about that and I leaned over and gave her a little kiss on her cheek, you know, and she kissed me back a little and then she said she had to get home, soak her tired feet, you know, they were sore, and I said, 'Let me rub them,' and she slid off one of her boots again and—"

He grabbed his napkin. Reese quickly handed him another,

almost knocking over the holder. Gavin blew his nose, balled the napkins up and tried to find a place on the table to set them. Arnie grabbed them. Set them in a mound to his right.

"What happened then?" Arnie asked, his voice steady.

"I don't know. It happened so fast. I mean, I thought she wanted to *do* something, like I said, and I, you know, shut down the motor and she said she couldn't be long or her dad would wonder where she was at, and then I—"

He hit the sides of his head with his fists.

Arnie pulled at Gavin's forearms, grabbed his fists. "Take your time, Gav. It's all right."

The grease was making Reese sick. Seeing that food, the sheen on those chops, the sticky feeling of that plastic tablecloth cover, the dust stuck to the salt and pepper shakers, made him all lightheaded. He took in a deep breath. Arnie's apartment was too dim, so different from Reese's own house with all its windows, its light. The rain pelted Arnie's tiny kitchen window, a branch tapped at it, for the wind was picking up. Reese had warned Arnie to get that oak trimmed back. Reese made sure each year to have his trees thinned out, dead branches taken down. The cobwebs from the light over the table to the ceiling blew around from some draft. Gavin's hitching, harder now, was upending Reese. He both wanted Gavin to tell them everything and wanted him to stop.

It was Arnie who urged him on. "You'll feel better if you just say it no matter what happened, okay?"

"Okay."

Why did that kid have to keep looking at him and nodding?

"Well, next thing I know she starts saying for me to get off her, like I'm hurting her or something, and I wasn't. I swear. I wouldn't hurt her." He rubbed his eyes, as if to clear his eyes to see that night again somehow. "And I do. I get halfway off her but she won't wait and she keeps saying, 'Get off me, get off me,' fixing her blouse back up, and I'm trying but she opens the door and tries to get out and I think my knee hit the gearshift or something, you know?" He pushed his plate a few inches away, ran a finger along the placemat, closed the cap on the ketchup. "Maybe popped it into neutral, you know?" His eyes were so red now, pleading for them to understand. "And since I was parked on a little slope, well, the truck started to coast backward and I didn't know, I didn't see, I didn't know it but she was under the truck—her boot got stuck and I don't know, like, she got twisted up somehow and the truck backed over her."

Arnie's face contorted and Reese wanted to say, "Arnie, stop!" But Reese felt his own face creasing hard like Arnie's. The girl might still be out there alive, in the rain, and so Reese had to ask, "Was she okay, or what?"

"No, no, no, no, no," Gavin said.

"Was she conscious?" Arnie asked, grabbing Gavin's forearm.

"No. She was dead. She was crushed. She was bleeding from her lips and her nose and, God, something coming out her ears and stuff, and I didn't want to move her but I had to move the truck and I don't know, I, I, I, the truck just, I just stalled it and the truck hopped and then coasted again and it pinned her. But she was dead already."

"Why didn't you call me, or 911, or someone?" Arnie asked.

"I don't know," he cried, pushing himself away from the table. "I don't even really remember what happened then, but there were headlights coming, off a little ways, but coming in my direction, and I pulled the truck away from her and lifted her into the bed and took off."

Gavin sat there, his head in his hands, his hair almost in his plate.

Arnie said, "You have to tell us where she's at so we can—"

"The dump. I rolled her up in a tarp and she's at the dump by the gas well on Toby Furnace Road."

Reese knew he should pick up the old phone waiting on Arnie's counter by Reese's mother's old pickle crock jam-packed full of spatulas and whisks. He should make the call to the police, but he couldn't seem to bring himself to move. He glanced across the table at Arnie watching him, his lips pursed. Reese grabbed his napkin, wiped his mouth. Gavin kept his head down, quietly sniffling.

Reese said, barely a whisper, "I can't."

And just like that, Arnie got up from the table, grabbed the phone. That damn refrigerator humming, that damn branch tapping at the window.

Arnie said, "Yes, hello, this is Arnie Couples and I, I want to report a, a, a body, where a body is located. Okay, okay, yes, Arnie, Arnold Couples, 127 Osprey . . ."

Gavin raised his head, rubbed his palms on his jeans. Reese wanted to hug the kid and slap him at the same time. Instead, he tried to soften his face, while they both listened to Arnie stumbling over his words, his voice giving out with every few syllables.

≈

Reese stood at the muddy perimeter of the dump area with Gavin, the lawyer Arnie called, and the sheriff just steps away from a cluster of police officers with their hands clasped behind their backs. Arnie had said he couldn't go along for the search. "Will you go?" "I will," Reese had said, grabbing Arnie, pulling him close, nearly knocking poor Arnie's glasses right off his face. He'd held him there until he could feel their hearts beating against each other's.

The excavator's bucket kept glancing off the side of an old refrigerator. Finally, it budged, tumbled away, exposing more coiled wire, pieces of drywall. It was drizzling and the air held the scents of all dumped things. Reese felt a tug at his elbow. It was Arnie. He'd come after all.

"Uncle Arnie," Gavin said. He held out his cuffed hand to touch Arnie's.

Reese leaned toward Arnie, whispered, "Good you're here."

Arnie stared straight ahead, gave one swift nod.

Suddenly, one of the men raised his arms and the operator stopped. The machine idled. Gavin leaned against Reese as the crew lifted something wrapped in a tarp, duct tape crisscrossing it.

Gavin took off toward it. Two deputies grabbed him. "Get him back," the sheriff yelled. They tackled him to the ground, pinned him there. Reese ran to him, stopped him from pounding his face on the ground. Arnie held his hands over his face, stood there like some sapling, his feet planted as if ready for a storm. Reese didn't know if he should get up and leave Gavin weeping in the mud, if he should run straight to Arnie and wrap his arms around him, if he should speed back to the restaurant and pull every single pair of red boots off every single one of his girls.

The operator got back in the cab of his machine, backed it away from the mess there. The deputies pulled Gavin from the ground. The sheriff held out a hand to help Reese up, but he waved him away, got up on his own.

Arnie had gotten into his car, was backing up. The headlights bounced as Arnie maneuvered his car over the rutted land and back onto the paved, smooth road again.

~

They didn't ID the body at the scene, but back at the medical examiner's office they made the confirmation. Ava Francine Singleton. Twenty-three. Wampum, Pennsylvania.

There was no evidence to put her in Gavin's truck. The kid knew how to clean up blood from all those months bleaching everything spotless at the restaurant, so his truck tires, the wheel wells, bed showed nothing. While they did have his confession, they couldn't have proven intent to harm or kidnapping. They charged him with two lesser crimes—involuntary manslaughter, obstruction—and Gavin's lawyer had him plead guilty so he wouldn't have to face trial. They talked mitigating circumstances, state of mind, and it helped that Ava's father—a man who looked even more like a shell of himself during the proceedings—didn't want a trial either. All parties agreed.

Reese stood in the courtroom beside Arnie while Gavin said, "Guilty." The judge asked him if he was forced to that plea. Gavin had to keep being reminded to speak into the microphone. It was one of the most difficult things Reese ever had to watch and he kept willing the kid to speak up so they wouldn't have to tell him again and again to move closer and closer.

The worst of it, though, was right after the body was found, when Reese had to tell the girls at the restaurant. They cried, hugged him, each one of them. He felt horrible, as if he'd run over Ava himself. He told the story over and over to his customers. And the looks on the faces of the crewmen, how one of them pulled out his hankie, wiped his nose, said, "Damn, that's rough. Poor kid." Reese didn't know if he meant Ava or Gavin.

Reese told the girls they could wear whatever shoes made them happy. He gathered up all the boots, stored them in the back room. Safely tucked away out of sight.

Some came in the next day in plain white Keds that got scuffed up after just one shift. Some found little ballerina-like black flats that made their feet look long and miserable when they did their dances, so Reese said they didn't have to do the dances anymore. He said they didn't even have to wear the uniforms, but the girls wanted to and kept up their dancing. Some wore these ugly red plastic shoes that looked like something a gardener would wear, with little do-dads stuck in them. Every customer that came in looked at the girls' feet. Most didn't make comments but some said, "Those comfortable?" When the girls answered, "Sure," the customers nodded and made their orders.

~

Weeks passed and Arnie wanted Reese to visit Gavin the first time at Camp Fisher prison.

As soon as they arrived, Gavin asked about the delivery runs, told Reese to say hi to everyone at work. Gavin kept it together until Arnie handed him the book on engines he wanted. That's when he kept saying how sorry he was. He cried a lot, and they both said "It's okay, bud" a lot.

When the guards guided Gavin back through those barred doors, Reese stood there watching him wave. The chipped paint on the bars was some sick shade of mint green. Made Reese's stomach hurt.

"He's gonna get eaten up in there," Arnie said. He fumbled around trying to strike his match to light up his cigarette as they walked to the car. What could Reese say?

On the way back Arnie and Reese talked business, got on the subject somehow about how everything was changing, how they had to keep reinventing their places, the way they had to always re-see their customers' needs. Arnie said Reese needed to think about offering free Wi-Fi. He said things were going great with the deal he'd made with that Heels and Healers group, how shocked he was at the number of truckers who came in for foot massages. That made them both laugh for a few seconds. But they quickly stopped, thinking of Ava. Arnie turned on the radio, changed stations, shut it back off. Reese adjusted the air vents, the visor. They passed three more exits, caught in thoughts they didn't want to share, Reese supposed.

Arnie said, "You decide yet what you'll do with those red boots."

Reese shook his head, rapped his knuckles on the window.

But Reese did know. People weren't ordering the special dance desserts they used to: the shimmy-shimmy-shakes, the line-dance pies, the square-dance sundaes. They weren't coming in for the birthday celebrations. Tips were decreasing daily.

They drove along the ugly stretch of the turnpike, the exit ramps and the median full of yellowed grass, the trees a dull green flanking all gray, and Reese noticed hawks sitting up high on the poles along that stretch of road. They passed five or six of them in just ten miles, looking down, down.

When Reese dipped his head to watch one dive, Arnie said, "You know they officially call them Highway Hawks now. Because there's so many."

"Got lots to feed on, I guess, huh?" Reese said.

"Mostly voles, more than we could count out there, I imagine." Arnie tapped the steering wheel. "We reinvented the grasslands with these expanses of roads, you know?"

It was so nice to notice the hawks like that, in a spot made for them—intentionally or not—on that stark stretch of road where rabbits and mice and other little creatures would have gotten asphalt-smeared unrecognizable had they ventured out, where songbirds' calls couldn't be heard anyway over the rumble of the tires, where their spreading of seed for pretty flowers wouldn't matter because crews would mow down everything growing anyway to keep the road clear, the signs unobstructed, the traffic always, always moving.

An Ever-Fixed Mark

"O no! it is an ever-fixed mark / That looks on
tempests and is never shaken;"
(Sonnet 116, Shakespeare)

One close summer evening, sky greening gray for strange weather, Western Pennsylvania Buckles and Beef proprietor Cecily Bargerstock walked around the lumpy-ass paddock through the dust-up haze, kicking everything that seemed uneven. All at once, wind lifted her hat, bits of hay and dirt splat her cheeks like spitballs. She stopped still, listened for a far-off tempest; it'd come first earlier in the day by way of her divorce lawyer asking, "How you gonna half a horse, Cecily? How you gonna split a pond in two?"

Cecily grabbed their best hand, Mick, and they gathered up everything that might have the sense to blow away, hunkered down in the half-dug cellar where Mick insisted they crawl to wait it out. Cecily held quiet while Mick messed with his damn rosary beads, mumbled shit nobody wanted to hear.

Cecily realized in her whole life she'd never wished up the idea of pummeled terrain, buildings coming down, cattle blown up into the skies, lost sheeting, tack strewn all over tarnation. But hell. Better to have the weather split it than to watch her soon-to-be ex walk up the path pointing to half of everything with those sore-looking bitten nails, those tender hands that held hers as they stood at the spot along the Sidle Creek right after he snugged his dead mother's emerald and diamond ring on her finger, saying, "I want us to be one forever," those tender hands that used to knead out the knurls in her back each night early on in their marriage, all the while him saying, "We're building up a life here together, Cee."

Cecily yelled to the low-ceilinged musty room, "Let gales gather up and blast through here. Leave nothing. Make it bare," and she ran up out of the cellar before Mick could stop her. She let the wind pull her every which way, sending her poor old head square into their pretty signpost her soon-to-be ex had painted that they'd planted into a hole they'd dug long ago, filled with concrete, shoring it up enough to handle any storm.

Oiling the Gun

*A*shes dangled on the end of Gwen's dad's cigarette. He squinted his eye as smoke drifted up. Tips of his fingers were slick with oil. The rifle lay on a bath towel on the green shag living room carpet, where one night before Gwen's cousins slithered disco moves to the Bee Gees "Night Fever." This late afternoon, no music. News yammered low. That story again about President Carter's daughter Amy and the elephant.

A year before, Gwen had been so envious of the girl and the baby elephant named Shanti she'd received "on behalf of the children of America." Gwen would never touch that elephant. She'd begged to visit their local zoo, but her dad said zoos were horrible places. "Keep beasts too far from their own ways of being in the world. Makes them all kinds of crazy."

The news now explained the story of Amy Carter and a "runaway elephant," spooked at Ethel Kennedy's home by a barking dog. Almost stampeded Amy. The secret service saved her.

Gwen's dad turned around quick to see the screen. He shook his head. He'd loved JFK. Hated Carter. He snapped his fingers to get Gwen's attention, threaded a cloth patch through the cleaning rod, slid the rod up through the barrel. The fawn chamois across his knees was stained with black ashes. She pushed closer so her knees were inches from the towel.

Tomatoes cooking down in a bath of basil, oregano, garlic bubbled in from the kitchen. Gwen's mom's scraping the pan's sides cut scratches in the sound of her humming gossip to Aunt Ramey. She peeked in to see Gwen was far enough from the gun, stretching the phone cord until the loops were near straight.

Gwen's dad was chatty, as always after a hunt. Three purpled squirrel bodies that had been soaking in the sink simmered in the sauce. They'd have spaghetti. She'd pretend again she wasn't hungry.

He explained the rifling, how careful one had to be with that rifling when cleaning the gun. His cigarette danced. He set it on the ashtray by his knees, picked up the gun, stared into the muzzle end of the barrel. Gwen gasped a little—eyes wide, a grin pushing at her dimples. Her gut dizzied.

"Don't hurt to look down it when it's empty," he said, "but you never should."

Gwen bit the inside of her cheek. She didn't want to hope the gun would go off, a bullet forgotten in the chamber. She didn't want to wonder what the house would sound like without him, if they'd sing louder, with more harmony, or if singing would stop altogether—after all, he was the best wailer of Hank Williams's "Long Gone Lonesome Blues." She didn't want to wonder if her brother would finally sleep sound instead of waking in the night, sleepwalking outside to check the beagles. He'd always made sure their dad hadn't beaten them for barking, for waking people who had the early shift. Would her brother be less or more skittish as the sole man left in the house?

She needed to get away from the gun, from all the possible worlds it offered. She tried to push her mind away from her house in The Slip, to think about only nice elephants, about strong arms of the secret service who could lift you from any danger, about girls with fathers who had more choices than her dad could ever have.

Gwen got up, walked to the kitchen. Sniffed at the sauce. Poked at the meat with the spoon. Watched it come loose from the bone.

Seeds

y wife leans into her pappy—Macon, she said yesterday—in
this photo we found folded in a hankie in a box next to a
creased paper and envelopes of dried seeds. We'd agreed she's five
then, though she didn't need me to concur, since she still had baby
teeth and it was before the scar on her forehead from the burn she
said she would get at seven.

Her tiny hands clutch the chamois shirt he wore that morning
before she went with her aunt Caroline. He'd probably just been
picking quince the color of the ribbon in her hair and sipping cool
spring water, and his mouth shows a stalled grin that hadn't yet
pursed into a committed and enduring frown.

His eyes stare. His arms don't cradle her. They don't know
how. They never would. Never had. He knew only how to plant
seeds and watch them grow—to plant a life and watch it live, thrive,
or die prematurely. He could bend and weed, graft even trees, and

deadhead; he could handle overripened tomatoes without bruising them, but he couldn't hold her without feeling as though he would explode, fall inside of himself, rot.

Her weight pushes him off-center, or was it the news he'd finally had no choice but to hear just before they said they were taking her? That it would be best for her, that he couldn't handle her without a mother to look over her. He hadn't really been invested, they said.

Or had he already heard that she would not recognize him when she turned fifteen and was beaten speckled plum by a stepfather, her aunt's poor choice of a new and flashy husband? Perhaps he felt in her that day an aching that would push man after man away in disgust of her neediness? He couldn't have known she'd meet me, who'd wanted someone to pot and hold dear in the sunlight on a sill so narrow as it was for her that she would need medicines, and doctors, and talking to keep just wide enough so as not to slip from.

He looks into the shutter like he might find her there instead of beside him. She might live forever, he thinks, in a happy picture, instead of this unhappy place that never seemed real after she, after both of them, were taken from him.

But he won't look to his right, at her, because he sees, by the way she breathes and waits for the camera to blink its indifferent eye, that she doesn't know that the little ride she's going on will be fifty years long without him, that she won't be permitted to see him at her mother's funeral two weeks later because, *Macon, it will be too hard on the girl.* So she, in anger, will not go to his funeral when she is sixty-seven. And she will call him by his first name, not

Pappy, even on the day before she, childless, married to me, dies of an empty uterus that grew cancer since it never could hold a child. *Why have children,* she said, when she met me at twenty-three, *when you only let them go.*

He doesn't want to give any of it away; he resists letting her fall into that knowledge. I think, from where I stand, that he was planning then he would leave the photo for her in a box with a broken rosary and a scratched diagram of a garden, with one baby tooth that was loosened just after the picture was taken. I told her that yesterday. And her same dashed eyebrows raised, and she smiled.

Licking the
Chocolate Glassine

If she pushes way back, she can remember the smell of Smitty: old man, dirt, grease, and gasoline. She can see his stubble, the snuff-spittled amber lines from the corners of his mouth, the way he lifted his hip to drag his bad leg across the tiny lot, and she can still hear the clug, clug, clug of the motors that won't give up after the key's turned off, and the heavy slam of the hood after Smitty checked oil and wiped his fingers on his dungarees, the rusty un-screwing of the gas caps. She can see the way the nozzle looked coming out of the ass ends of those cars, just where the license plate hinged.

Those were odd and even days. Gas rationing. Late '70s. She can see the roll of cash Smitty'd pull from his pocket and thumb through for change. She can see hints of the Smitty Crew's faces; she clearly sees their hairy legs and Converses. She sees the worn bench butted up against the outside wall of the service station where they sat and carved marijuana leaves on the bench, and their initials, and words she wasn't allowed to say. She sees their pen knives.

Those boys were in their late teens, and one of her friends back then had insisted they hung out at Smitty's because they could steal snuff and cigs, claimed they'd rigged the cola machine.

She worries now if those boys were kind to Smitty, if they really called him names like her friend had insisted they did all those years ago—"They call him gimpy Smitty. 'Cause he can't walk right. It's all right. Everyone calls him that and everyone steals from him. He doesn't care." Even then she hadn't believed this. Or had she?

She wants to remember it correctly, because that old friend has just since died and she can no longer ask him.

She still hears the Smitty Crew's whispers and chuckles when she asked for Bit-O-Honeys and Sugar Daddies and Mary Janes. They were rapt with inside jokes she and her girlfriends didn't yet get because they were eleven, flat-chested, and scared of the boys.

Now she understands why their smutty words seared into her head, why she believed them when they said Bubble Yum was so soft because it was made with spider eggs. Why she dreams, even now, of a mouthful of gum she can't gag out fast enough.

Now she understands why that place, those boys, drew her in, why she could get talked into stealing a Reese's from the shelf. She had to prove she was more than eleven, more than a goody-goody, more than a girl.

She can still see Smitty's eyes as he filled the poke with the Tootsie Rolls she actually bought as a distraction so her friends could swipe more. She can still feel that stolen Reese's press on her side, the corners of its packaging gouging her skin, while he counted. She can still feel how the wood floor slanted, see how the light bulb above the register was sprinkled with dust, how Smitty's eyes were clouded over with what she knows now were cataracts, but *then* worried were the eyes of God looking straight through her.

But she can't recall Smitty's voice. Another friend from that day who she's called to ask about old Smitty insists he stuttered, but she can't retrieve it however much she tries. She only sees his nod when she hands him enough to pay for the Tootsie Rolls only.

She wants to go back. Far back in time. She wants to get off her hand-me-down bike, walk through the hot sun, through the cloud of exhaust, past the Smitty Crew, and back into the cool mustiness of the service station. She wants to tuck the Reese's back on the shelf, line it up edge to edge with the others so Smitty will never know she took it. She wants to stick around a little. Ask him how he's doing? What makes him happy? What he wants out of life? She wants to listen to see if he stutters because she'll be patient. She won't make fun. She understands from her own speech classes how it feels when your mouth betrays you. Hers is a lisp. She wants to thank him for selling candy, for keeping stock of orange pop and Coke, for giving them more candy than their bottle returns were worth, for trusting them. Because now she sees that he did trust them. All of them. And they took such advantage of him in countless ways. Never really thanked him.

But she can't go back. Instead, she feels the burning sting on her knees and she sees the blood taking its time to rise up through her dust-covered skin after she'd wrecked her bike getting away from what she'd done.

And she can still feel, against her tongue, the chocolate glassine paper that held that melted mess she licked off clean while laughing with the others at how stupid Smitty was. She can still see the muddied ground under the maple where they unloaded the bounty from their shirts and shorts and socks, the mess of bright labels against that part of the ground that wouldn't grow grass, for the shade kept the sun from ever hitting it.

The Steep Side

The boy rode up the steep gas line path on his new dirt bike, crested the hill, and found the sounds. These cries from two hills over, above the idling of his bike, hadn't been those of a fox or hawk or dying whitetail. Now he saw their root: the woman on the ground, her shirt pulled up, another woman crouched beside her.

He started to say, *Is she okay?* But the air got heavy, his helmet felt too snug. There was a new heat and pressure in his eyes so he pulled his goggles up over his visor. He shut down the bike. Crows barked. Cicadas whined.

～

Looking down from a cloudless blue, through the tippy-top leaves of the elms and oaks to the rutted ground, one would spot this trio made up of a boy on his bike and two women who don't live in the valley. The boy is at least three bike lengths away. One of the women is mightily pregnant. She's short, all baby, with willowy arms and spikey black hair, a ruddy face, a diamond nose piercing that glitters in the sun, and lots of rings on the fingers of her right hand that's spread wide across her belly, touching where blood's weeping from her. The other has two inches of brown roots on her head of long, ponytailed, bleached-blond hair. A few loops of hair have come loose. She's thick through her middle, has braces on her teeth.

She tells the boy she's a nurse. She's wearing what might be scrubs or pajama bottoms.

In these parts you smell the noxious invasive multiflora rose busy weighing down the trees, leaching into riparian strips along the Sidle. You see the brand-new minivan clashing this space, its rear door slid open. You hear the old Farmall H tractor Miles McIntyre has restored. Sound here carries in disorienting ways— bending around and between trees, echoing off once-stripped hillsides.

This path they're on is an open green swath amidst tall timber—a natural gas pipeline right-of-way—remote but accessible by vehicle. On this particular easement, the ground is uneven. Driving a low-clearance vehicle is a mistake.

～

He can't be more than fifteen. A tall fifteen. She must explain the screaming that stopped as soon as he shut down his bike.

She says, *I'm helping her.*

He doesn't nod. He doesn't move.

Her tools are shiny. The sun wants to catch the silver of them, to give her up, but the sky clouds over.

≂

Later in the evening, after the women are gone, the boy will return to the gas line with his dad and an investigator wearing glasses that have speckles on the lenses and who has a slight limp when he walks.

They'll take a different route than the boy took the first time. The boy will ride his dirt bike, geared down and lugging. His father and the investigator will follow in his dad's pickup. They'll see where the woman's minivan dragged over a high spot on the crowned section of the path that's been rutted out by rain.

They'll say, *This is the way she came in.*

The boy will sit up straighter on his bike. He'll hang his helmet on his bars, scratch his shoulder. He'll feel some sense of direction with them there, like he's an excerpt from the cloudless part of this story. And when his father tells this story again and again, the boy will always make sure to add the detail about how the minivan dragged over that spot, how the undercarriage had clay and high grass stuck to it. And his dad will nod and he'll nod back. That detail will always be exactly right, not bleary or liquid.

≂

The older woman said, *We were just taking a ride and she wanted to get out and walk a little. Just carsick.* She pushed her bloodied hand on the dirt, stood up. She wiped that same hand on her pants. He didn't see the knife. She hid it. They both looked at the smear, maroon-like, on the pastel blue material at her right thigh. Then they both looked at the pregnant woman juddering on the ground who didn't say a word and didn't peer into the boy's eyes like the older woman did. She kept hers shut until the woman-who-said-she-was-a-nurse repeated something about a ride, about taking a rest, and that's when the pregnant woman opened her eyes slightly, gazed only at the boy's bike, his boots, tried to reach for him.

~

He's seen people gutting things in the woods before, their bloodied hands, the stains on their jeans or camos where they've wiped their hands for lack of a rag. He's smelled this tinny smell. His father has always used latex gloves with deer. Ticks. Lyme.

~

The boy will not go out for small game in the fall. He'll miss archery altogether. In the winter, when snow lays down a blanket for easy tracking, he'll walk this path again and then he'll stop coming here for a long while no matter the season.

~

That's my car, the woman-who-said-she-was-a-nurse said to the boy. She pointed her finger off to the far left, near what might have been a patch of mountain laurel. Her blue-green minivan shadowed, masked by a thick stand of trees, its hot engine ticking.

~

The boy's arms are cement—not just from arm pump, from riding too tight, fighting the bike that's not set up yet for his weight and skill level. He shakes them loose. The bike feels heavy between his legs, feels like it might push him over to one side or another, and he's hoping it will restart with one kick. It's a YZ250 four-stroke—he's new to it, having only ever ridden a smaller CR125 two-stroke—and sometimes it takes many kicks to restart when it's hot. His dad has warned him about this. His dad has warned him about arm pump, too, has explained the newfangled surgery some motocross pros are rumored to have opted for that removes the fascia from their forearms to keep from experiencing this pooling of blood.

Gotta stay loose, his father says all the time. *Always relax when you're out riding. And don't let much time go between rides. Stay in shape, that's all.*

Yes, the boy's arms are cement now, and his legs. Not from riding at all. From thinking about the places this pregnant woman's skin's been cut through. He doesn't want to look closer.

≈

He'll tell his dad about the minivan first when he gets back home. Before he takes off his gloves and helmet, his words will muffle through the mouthguard, his eyes will shift focus from his dad's face to the hill, to the trees, and back, and his dad will say what he always says, *Slow down.*

His dad will grab his .38, call 911, back the four-wheeler out of the machine shed.

≈

The older woman said to the boy, *We're good friends.* The pregnant woman on the ground didn't nod. She leaned on one elbow, kept her splayed hand on her full tight belly, which showed bare-naked above her partly pulled down shorts. A little strip of her bra was bright white next to her flowered shirt. The shirt, jam-packed with red and pink flowers, shocked all the green surrounding her body.

~

The well tender has kept the path unobstructed so he can do regular checks. On this day, the path is passable, but the growth's knee-high and that's likely why the boy cannot see all the blood yet.

~

The woman-who-calls-herself-a-nurse walks toward the boy, positions herself between him and the pregnant woman on the ground. That milky white part of her scalp between those dark roots is also made of white hair, about a quarter inch of it, splitting the middle of her head.

~

He's too scared to ask questions. He may just turn around, ride off somewhere. A yammer of another bike, way off, cuts through the trees. *You out riding with friends?* she asks, and when he doesn't answer, she says, *That's a nice bike.*

~

He'll sell the bike at the end of summer.

When he sees the kid he's sold it to racing it at a local track next spring in the second Schoolboy Moto, pulling a hole shot, nearly wrecking at the checkered but placing second, he'll try not to let these women bloom up in his head again. He'll try to find the kid in the pits, ask him about the suspension, how the bike's been running. Which oil does he use? Amsoil or Klotz?

⌁

He hoped someone else would come upon them. But he knew better because this was one of the most remote gas lines in the valley. He rarely saw tire tracks, long ruts, from other bikes.

He stood there, tried to pretend the tiny sounds flowing up from the woman on the ground were from some song she was humming and not whimpers like his dog made when a coal truck nipped and spun her on the road last summer, when they tried to stabilize her leg with a wooden shim and strips of his dad's worn handkerchief, even though they both knew the dog's major organs were broken, too.

⌁

When he's in his mid-twenties and still dreaming about these two women, still seeing the younger woman's body turn slightly to reveal the two cuts—one splitting her middle straight down from her belly button, the other edging through her dark pubic hair, the two creating an upside-down dark red T—half the ash trees that line this swath will have fallen, crisscrossing the path. The emerald ash borer will have taken them down.

⌁

When she said, *You should get back to your ride, huh? It's a great day for it,* and raised her arms toward the canopy's light blue opening, he kicked the starter and in four, five, maybe eight kicks, it finally lit up. He took off the way he came. Down over the gas line. He shortcutted across Delmar Blackwell's field, not caring if he was running through newly planted crops, not caring if he hit groundhog holes, not worrying about winding out the gears too far or how much head shake he was getting or whether or not he should take the township road or if he spun limestone on his dad's truck as he flew past it and skidded to a stop at the barn, and he didn't care about laying the bike on its side, about gas leaking out onto the ground through the overflow, about the stones scratching the virgin plastic number plate so deep.

∽

She knows when she hears the bike again, and this time melded with other clamors—a rumbling four-wheeler, and the yelling, *Hey, hey,* by a man who is the boy's father—her plan is wrecked. It's over.

She isn't having the baby she wants, the baby she's been lying about carrying in her own womb fixed to her by its cord, the baby that can restore the other one she's told her husband is still growing inside her body. She's having this one, though.

The pregnant woman tries to crawl away from her toward the sounds of the approaching bike, pulling at clumps of tall grass that break off or uproot, calling out *Please, please,* getting no more than inches away for the gap in her hemorrhaging middle.

∽

Years from now, when his wife is prepped for her spinal nerve block and then eased back onto the table, when the surgeon says, *You two ready to see your baby?* and he hears the tap-buzz, tap-buzz of the laser, sees the smoke—not something he could have imagined—rising from his wife's smooth skin, swirling above the sunset-orange betadine, the boy will try to misremember the image of the woman's slashed swollen belly. He'll close his eyes, he'll have to. When he opens them he'll have his son in his arms. He'll cry for himself, for the two women and that child, that child who survived that day and lived, lived.

⁓

His father backed the woman away from the other with the threat of his outstretched arms, his gun, and knotted her wrists together with the nylon drag rope they always used for large game. He told the boy to ride back, fast, to the barn. Meet the ambulance, show them the way in. *Don't have them take the steep side,* his father said.

⁓

The boy's an avid motocrosser in a place where houses spatter instead of drench the landscape, where dirt bike riders have utilized these maintained, seemingly remote paths as connections from field to timber, from parcel to parcel, for decades. The steepest sections are their hill climbs. There are over two hundred Marcellus gas wells in the county, which means there are hundreds of these paths.

And hunters of grouse, ring-necked pheasants, squirrel, and larger game—black bear and whitetail—walk these paths to steer clear of tangles of poison oak and ivy, of brambles so big they can slice through jeans.

⁓

He will never ride his bike this effortlessly again, hitting each rut with perfect timing. He's riding over his head. He's racing.

He will never again speak to people in the medical community with such authority about what he's seen and heard. Slowly, eloquently, effectively.

He will remember, though, how that ambulance looked to him, over his shoulder as he led it, how it rocked, heaved, how its engine bawled but kept coming.

He will remember the two men in blue and black emergency uniforms, one short and bald with an eagle tattoo on his forearm, one taller with a chafed neck and thick glasses who kept shaking his head.

He will remember how his father sat on a moss-covered log next to that tied-up woman, held his arm up across her chest like he held an arm across the boy's chest when he hit the brakes too hard in the truck.

He will remember how one of the uniformed men called for a helicopter, how they both talked in warm, slow words to the woman on the ground as one untangled the looped tubing, placed the oxygen mask over her nose and mouth, how their voices clipped and bit as the paramedic threaded two IVs into her arms, how they yelled out, as they packed the white gauze into her gaping belly, *Stay with us. Come on, now. Stay with us*, how they quickly lifted her into the ambulance, how it bumped down the hill to the open field, how the helicopter's turbine squealed, how, when it took off, bits of Delmar Blackwell's newly seeded ground lifted with it.

~

The boy washed his bike with the power hose, careful not to get water in the exhaust, pulled the long grass from where it tangled in the foot pegs, in the chain. He changed the filter. He rewired his grips. He set his helmet on the shelf, picked the dried mud-splatter off his riding gear until he saw more than mud spots.

He rolled up the gear, threw the bundle on the pile of dirty laundry, ran up to his room and shut the door. He stared at the posters of motocross champions airborne over triples, or scrubbing jumps, or hitting turns, roosting the crowd with dirt. Then he buried his head in his pillow.

~

The woman-who-calls-herself-a-nurse gives her very detailed statement, says she didn't want to harm the baby so she gave the young woman crushed-up benzodiazepines in her orange juice just to make her loopy enough to get her into the van. She says she didn't think she'd come to until after she finished. She says she planned to stitch her back up. She says she had sutures. She says she ordered them online. She writes it all out on a yellow legal pad and signs it.

She's fingerprinted and handcuffed and evaluated by one psychologist and then another and to everyone, even the guards, even her cellmate, she asks if the young boy on the bike is okay, if she can talk to him. She says she feels she may have frightened him. She says she didn't mean to scare anyone.

~

The pregnant woman will deliver a healthy girl with thick black hair within minutes of getting to the hospital. The baby will have a high Apgar score. She'll grow up, go off to college and study soil engineering. She'll research the effects of fracking. She'll marry an arborist.

~

The boy rode only on practice tracks the summer after he found those two women in the woods—man-made excavated tracks on open fields, padded with mulch, loamy berms. He didn't hill-climb up the gas well right-of-ways with friends or by himself, feeling the bike pull him up the steep lines.

~

The boy drives the township road in his dad's pickup, sometimes past the entrance where the well tender keeps it open, wide. Runoff puddles in the ruts and sometimes seeps out onto the road. There must be a spring up there, up where they, all three, once found themselves together.

~

The boy, grown into a man, will walk back there one day with his son, searching for leaves of one of the remaining ash trees for his seventh-grade science project. His son will stop near the crest of the hill and say, *It's really pretty up here, Dad*. He'll watch his son's hands run over the bark of the trees that line the path. He'll scan the wood line for a healthy ash and look, too, for the spot, but he won't be able to locate it. There will be no markers. The mayapples will inch out onto the path and everything will be hues of green.

Acknowledgments

Thank you, my incredible agent, Nicole Cunningham, and The Book Group, for finding me through my stories, believing in them, and giving me the best gift, your support and tenacious we-won't-give-up attitude, for being exacting, strategic, and always reminding me to live my whole life.

Thank you, my super-editor, Carl Bromley, for taking a chance on this collection, for expertly fine-tuning it, for—along with the whole dedicated, stellar Melville House team—helping me feel I was never alone in this publishing world, for always signing off with "Cheers!"

This book would not be possible without the hard workers I've interviewed, watched, worked alongside. Your words are important, melodious, beautiful, and they belong in books.

With gratitude for the financial support of the Georgia Court Faculty scholarship, Greater Pittsburgh Arts Council, Tinker Mountain Writers Workshop, and Vermont College of Fine Arts

Work Study program, and my great appreciation to all the editors who've provided original homes for my work as well as the marvelous authors who read advanced copies, wrote such generous blurbs.

I would love to include names of every one of my friends, fellow writers, colleagues, students who've inspired me, who've helped me stay the course. The list is long. But I'd be up at 3 am in a flurry of worry that I'd forgotten someone if I tried to name each of you. You know who you are.

Profound thanks to East Franklin, KJHS, KHS teachers for opening up my world to stories, written, drawn, spoken, sung, and IUP professors for your literary theory/analysis classes, for introducing me to, and being, my literary heroes. To my VCFA postgraduate instructors for blazing a path through the densest writing-world-thicket, especially fiction faculty, Ellen Lesser, Lee Martin, Billy Giraldi, Andre Dubus III, for helping me find my voice, and many, many thanks, David Jauss, for your brilliant editorial savvy in the VCFA mentorship program and beyond, for your steady crafting even when I was truly screwing things up. To flash instructors Kathy Fish, Nancy Stohlman, Sherrie Flick for your unsurpassed talent. To Clare Beams and Barbara Jones for your wisdom. To my excellent beta readers, advisers: Lauri Grotstein, Susan Thibadeau, Linda Niehoff, Gale McGloin, Margaret Whitford, Meredith Mileti, Joann Kielar, Marc Nieson, Michelle Belan, Windy Lynn Harris, Jan Elman-Stout, Rebecca Drake, Nancy Martin, Helena Rho, Terri Bourke, April Bradley, Heather Aronson, Pat Hart, Maureen McGranaghan, Many Ly.

And many thanks to the wheeze-laugh-'til-we-cry Dewey Hall Crew and all great VCFA friends; my ace fellow editors at *jmww Journal*; my hard-working colleagues at Duquesne, Chatham; the Quills and Jennifer Kircher Herman; John Lugo-Trebble and Story-Talk; so many outstanding Word Tango workshop partners; Linda Cunningham, Kittanning Public Library's book club, and my awesome lecture partner, Sandy Bradigan; fellow Pittsburgh Sisters-&-Sibs-in-Crime members; the aptly named Friendship writing group who met, yes, in Friendship; the lovely, one-of-a-kind Fishtank, Paul Beckman's F-Bomb KGB Bar Red Room pals; Tammy, Kellie, Jamie, you've given me the best advice while I've sat in your salon chairs; Michelle and Lissa for all of our heart-to-hearts; the best neighbors a person could ever ask for; Diane, Jackie, Susan; countless Twitter friends, up at all hours, always offering me inspiration and kindness; my dearest comrades around the world, the Wordfishers, who've answered questions and bolstered me in times of great stress!

Deepest gratitude to Dr. Deborah West and Carol Hughes for adding skills to my toolkit when PTSD took me far away from my teaching and writing mind. You saved me many, many times. Thank you Mrs. Edith Yates, for the honor of being your caregiver. I loved your stories. Cheryl Focht, thank you for the support, kindness, and care for Liam, for me. Many thanks to Sister Mary Hall, for her encouragement and tireless work for social justice. My mentor, Carole Bencich, thank you for continuing, long after I was in your classroom, to teach me.

I'm so thankful to my family, my parents, Libby Jo (Booher) and the late Joe Recupero, for providing the table around which so many storytellers gathered for food, drink, smokes, and understanding. You invited characters of all kinds into our home. You sang songs together and taught me to sing, too, and you taught us kids to harmonize! You reminded me how to work hard, look for signs, and that life goes well beyond what we can touch, see, hear.

Further thanks to the entire McIlwain family, for welcoming me into your wonderfulness, your contagious laughter, your loving hearts, for sharing with me your beach weeks, bar nights, egg hunts, hilarious phrases, and for giving us the stunning space among the trees and creeks where we could begin, thrive, and continue our creative lives.

Thank you to my husband, my partner, my dear Thomas, for coming home from digging dirt each day and telling me, "Hey, I have a story for you," for not allowing me to ever give up, for saying, when I most needed to hear it, "You can do this. I know you can." For giving me so much to live for and laugh about and linger in. You are the best of my past, my present, my future.

Thank you to my amazing son, Liam, for believing artists have a solid place in this world, for teaching me how to be brave, to be in the moment, to practice self-care, and to send good energy into the universe, for sharing with me a language that is all your own. You are my center.